You'll Find Me in Manhattan

JILL KNAPP

Harper
impulse
we've got the love

Harper*Impulse* an imprint of
HarperCollins*Publishers* Ltd
1 London Bridge Street
London SE1 9GF

www.harpercollins.co.uk

A Paperback Original 2015

First published in Great Britain in ebook format by Harper*Impulse* 2015

A catalogue record for this book is
available from the British Library

ISBN: 9780008122843

Automatically produced by Atomik ePublisher from Easypress

Printed and bound in Great Britain

JILL KNAPP

I'm a native New Yorker who now lives in North Carolina with
wo amazing dogs. I was actually inspired to start writing
els from watching television of all things. There were these
azing shows I watched growing up and I thought if I could
create a story that touched people the way that these stories
e touched me, I would accomplish my goal.

art from my novels, I have been published in magazines,
wspapers, and other websites including The Huffington Post
d HelloGiggles. I am also the Features Editor for the online
agazine HomeMade Bride.

addition to writing, I hold an M.A in Psychology and taught
the college level for three years.

www.jillknappzitron.com

@JL_Knapp

For everyone who believes in soul-mates,
true love, and forever.

He adored New York City. He idolized it all out of proportion…he romanticized it all out of proportion. Yes. To him, no matter what the season was, this was still a town that existed in black and white…

Woody Allen

Prologue

"Amalia?" he muttered my name as usual, never to be said with full strength. But something was different this time. He wasn't using the familiar judgmental tone I had become accustomed to.

"At the end of it all, it's just you you're left with," he continued. "Some people say life is short, and there's no denying that." He glanced down at the picture on his desk for a moment, taking a deep breath in the process. "But life is also *long*." He looked up from the photo, and his eyebrows popped up like two arrows on his forehead. "*Too* long to choose a path that will lead you nowhere. Much too long not to follow your heart."

As he took a step closer to me, I could feel tears forming in the back of my eyes. But it didn't matter. I was stronger now. But still not strong enough to know what to say.

"I wish I had known sooner," he muttered in a near-whisper. "But you still have time. You have a *choice*."

Didn't I always? But when have I chosen wisely? I could feel the side of my lip pulling my face into a grimace. He didn't seem to notice.

"Don't choose poorly," he shook his head. If I looked close enough, I could see the sparkle of tears beginning to form in his brown eyes.

I turned my head away and reached for the door, but it was no use. His words had already penetrated something deep inside me. Perhaps it was something I had known all along.

I could almost hear Autumn's voice gloating in my head.

In psychology this is referred to as a "breakthrough."

One – Amalia

"Amalia, wait!" Hayden called out from behind me. I could hear his voice cracking with distress beneath each syllable.

Despite his unease, probably brought on by chasing me in a foot pursuit, he was handling himself pretty well. Unlike me, his breath seemed perfectly in sync. I guess that's the difference between a well-toned, six-foot-something guy running, and a five-foot five-inch girl who hasn't been to the gym since 2010. I took a small moment to commend myself on not being a smoker and wondered how Olivia would he holding up in the exact same situation.

Although something told me Olivia wouldn't be running through the crowded streets of midtown to get away from Alex. Or maybe she would, she did run away during the NYU dinner and that was in the financial district. Come to think of it, I never asked her why she did that. I assumed it was because of something Alex had done, or said, to her.

That seemed like a lifetime ago.

Not really paying attention to where I was headed, I somehow managed to run, in high heels no less, right into the middle of the most heavily populated area in Manhattan. Times Square.

Jackpot.

It was mean, I know. But he was following me, and I had to lead him somewhere he wouldn't be able to catch up with me. I had to do something harsh, something drastic.

I had to get him to hate me.

Bustles of children with their parents zipped around me as the giant flashing billboards with advertisements for Broadway shows suddenly distracted me and had me wondering if I, in fact, would somehow get trapped in one of these novelty stores for the next two hours. Or, at least, until Hayden stopped chasing me.

"Amalia!" he puffed out. "Please!" Traces of panic and panting tickled his voice.

He was getting closer. I picked up the pace and accidentally collided with a street artist making caricatures of a neighboring couple. I slowed my speed to regain my footing, all the while observing their unspoken comfort with one another. Even with me literally crashing through their afternoon activities, they laughed it off and held hands. I mumbled that I was sorry and I shook my head, while tears threatened to spill out of my already puffy eyes.

I dodged past yet another crowd of people dressed warmly in heavy down coats, laughing, ignoring the punishing cold of February in the city. My favorite magenta-colored wool scarf had flown off my neck a few blocks back. But as cold as it was, I was drenched in sweat from my sprint. Finally, I stopped running and ducked behind the large red staircase pavilion: a hideous eyesore in Times Square that opened in 2008. I couldn't believe how thankful I was to see it right at this very moment. The giant bleacher-like structure allowed tourists to have a seat and take in the scenery. But right now, I wanted to let it all out. Force it all out. Everything I was feeling. I ducked further down, my skinny jeans stretching in all the wrong places as I uncomfortably made myself smaller. I took a deep breath, which sounded somewhere in between a gasp and a sob, and pressed the palms of my hands into my eyes. I knew I seemed like a crazy person, but better he thought that than continued to see me as perfect.

Perfect. The word still echoed with me. The last real conversation we had before I told him I was choosing Michael. The last conversation before Michael's deadline. After today, Hayden would surely never feel that way about me again. But wasn't that what I wanted?

My palms were wet and covered in smeared mascara. I wiped them on my dark wash jeans, not caring about any make-up stains that might ensue in the process. I knew I looked borderline homeless, or maybe like a mental patient who had escaped from a nearby hospital. But right now I was really grateful that I was in New York City. You could have yourself convinced that you were the craziest person this side of the Hudson River, but some loon was always nearby, challenging you for the title.

I took a couple of more deep breaths, my chest rising and falling so hard I had to unzip my puffy down jacket. I gently pressed my fingertips into the pulse point in my neck and willed my heart to slow down. A beat later, my phone buzzed in my purse. I jumped from anxiety and then moved my hand from my neck to my chest. I really needed to calm down. Slowly, I reached into my bag for my phone, handling it like it was a bomb about to explode. Hayden's name lit up on the screen in the form of a text message. I hesitantly unlocked my phone, bracing myself for the inevitable flash of anger. A message charged with hate and disdain for me.

But it wasn't. And somehow that made it even worse.

Amalia – I don't understand, but I guess I don't need to. You chose someone else and I have to respect that. Don't worry, I won't chase you anymore. But I can't promise I'll stop loving you.
   H

I glanced down at the ground for a moment before slowly tucking the phone back into my purse. A chilling breeze blew through my disheveled hair, and, just like that, I was freezing again. Still unable to move, I just sat on the ground of Times Square for a few more seconds. I couldn't move, I couldn't blink, couldn't process a single thing.

Then I screamed. I don't think anyone heard me, it's always so loud in that part of the city, but I still screamed. I screamed and cried, and screamed some more. I screamed so loudly and for so long, that my voice felt and sounded metallic when I finished.

I had no idea how much time passed, but when my legs finally felt strong enough to move I walked up to the corner of 7th avenue and hailed a cab back to my neighborhood, Murray Hill. I numbly stared out the window the entire car ride and gazed at everyone mindlessly walking around. Scurrying along at lightning speed to get to their next meeting or to their lunch plans, or nowhere at all. Just trained like animals to rush through their life out of desperate fear that might miss something *important*.

That was the first time I really allowed myself to feel it. The first time I truly thought: I have to get out of New York.

Two – Olivia

Four months later

"I don't know how I feel about this one," I smoothed the silky bodice with my right hand, while trying to wrap the alarmingly long crystallized train in my left. "It's a bit too much dress for me."

The room was cold and I shivered while standing in the gown. Although it was only the end of May, the manager of this establishment had the air-conditioning on the highest possible setting. Which made it pretty darn uncomfortable to stand in a sleeveless dress. If only to make this afternoon with my mother more pleasant.

As soon as I caught Amalia's eye, she grimaced. I could tell from that one look that she completely agreed. The train had to be somewhere near four feet long. Too long even to just take pictures in! I didn't even want to check the price tag. Then my eyes fell on to my mother, who was already making her way over to me.

"Well, darling, it is your wedding day," she spoke in a stern voice through a tight, fake smile. She tucked a piece of her short brown hair behind her ear and looked me square in the eyes. "When else will you get to dress up like a princess?" She crossed her arms in front of her, challenging me. I had no idea why she cared so much.

I lowered my eyebrows and shook my head. I didn't really feel like that was entirely the point of finding the right wedding dress. I was standing on a small podium in front of a giant mirror with two supporting mirrors on each side, allowing me to see this giant, glitter-covered cupcake from every angle. I hadn't even booked the venue for my nuptials yet, but my mother had insisted that we grab the first appointment we could get at Wedding Atelier on Madison Avenue. Apparently, the average bridal gown called for three alterations, taking anywhere from three weeks to three months in between visits. I made a mental note to really watch my weight during this next year. You can always take the dress in, but you certainly can't add more material.

I still couldn't believe I would be getting married and graduating from my Master's program in the same year. A smile tugged on my mouth as I remembered Alex's perfect proposal to me on New Year's Eve. But just as quick as it brushed my lips, the smile faded and the anxiety of school nestled its way back into my chest. I was hoping that working with Dr. Greenfield would help prepare me for what I was going to do after graduation. Or at the very least, guarantee one letter of recommendation. I had narrowed down the application process to three Ph.D. programs, all in New York. I tried to talk to my mom about how overwhelmed I felt, but instead of lending an ear, she convinced me to get the wedding planning out of the way so I could focus on school when it was all sorted out. I could tell she was much more interested in my wedding than my career path. She finally gave me enough anxiety on the matter that I caved and reluctantly agreed to let her come with me. I played the "maid of honor card," asking Amalia to come along as a buffer.

"I understand it's *my* wedding day," I emphasized the word *my*. "I just don't think this is the right dress for me. I want something a little less," I paused, searching for the right word. "Overwhelming."

I looked to Amalia for help, and with the smallest nod I knew she completely understood what I was talking about. She walked over to the sales associate that had been helping us and whispered something in her ear. I wondered if she was trying to come up with a plan to have my mother kicked out of the store.

My mother let out an exaggerated sigh and downed the rest of her complimentary champagne. She then turned to a different sales associate and gently shook her empty champagne flute, indicating that she'd like a top-off. I shook my head and wished my dad could be here instead of her, but she had insisted this was a "*woman thing*," and wouldn't have it any other way.

A beat later, Amalia and a dark-haired sales associate came strutting over to us holding a rack of more suitable and demure wedding gowns. I felt a smile tug on the side of my lips, while my mother's morphed into a purse.

"That one," Amalia pointed to lace-covered gown and the sales associate quickly held it up and smiled, patiently waiting for my approval. I eyed the gown. It was nothing short of magnificent. There were slim, tank-like sleeves that were completely made of Chantilly lace, the neckline fell into a sweetheart style, but not too plunging. The rest of the gown was silk with an overlay tastefully covered in the same lace as the sleeves, and the train was even a manageable length.

"May I see the back of the dress?" I took a step off the podium and walked closer to the gown.

The back of the dress was low-cut. Stylish with a hint of sexy. I wouldn't be able to wear a bra with the gown, but most brides had one sewn in anyway. From the waist down to the beginning of the train were about thirty satin-covered buttons. I put my hand on my chest, unable to speak for a moment. I felt a small stream of tears flow into my eyes as I imagined marrying Alex in that dress, and didn't even try to stop them from coming out. I hadn't put on any make-up out of fear that I'd somehow manage to smudge some on the dresses and owe fifteen thousand dollars in gowns.

"I'd like to try that on," I whispered through a sniff, feeling a slight rush of excitement. Amalia winked and smiled back. "Can you come into the dressing room with me and help me with the buttons?"

Amalia touched her fingertip to her lips, pretending to contemplate this task. "I do believe that is a job for the maid of honor," she pretended to brush some dust off her shoulders and laughed.

The red-headed sales associate with the champagne bottle came back to fill up my mother's glass. She slowly sat back down on the plush couch and crossed her legs. "I'm not sure how that will look, but by all means try it on. We haven't anything better to do today." She checked her Movado watch and then looked back up at me.

I pressed my mouth into a tight-lipped smile, growing more impatient with her callousness. "Oh, if I'm keeping you, Mother, please don't feel obligated to stay." Before I could gauge her reaction, Amalia grabbed the long train of the sparkle disaster I was still wearing and motioned for me to follow her into the dressing room.

Once we were alone, I let out a small grunt. This was supposed to be a wonderful moment, and my mother was nearly ruining it.

"You're mom's kind of a handful," Amalia muttered with wide eyes. Her phone buzzed in her jean pocket, but she ignored it.

"Do you need to get that?" I answered as she helped me out of the first dress. I took a step back and admired the perfect gown I was about to try on and allowed myself to do a little dance in my bra and underwear.

Amalia laughed. "Nice moves. But you should save it for your honeymoon. And, no, I don't need to get it, it's probably Michael. He knows I'm with you, maid-of-honor duties and all. I'm having dinner with him later."

"So this is really happening, then?" I asked as I held my arms over my head so she could help me into the dress. "You and Michael are officially dating?"

Amalia stood on the tiny stool in the dressing room and helped pull the gown over my head, after which she motioned for me to turn around so she could get started on the exuberant amount of buttons.

"Leave it the girl in the wedding gown to ask me if Michael and I were really happening!" she rolled her eyes. "I think your wedding is a *much* bigger deal than me and Michael going out to dinner."

"It's a big deal!" I teased. "While I may be getting married at the age of twenty-five, I still find the idea of you and Michael having a genuine relationship more shocking."

"Well, don't die of shock just yet," she started. "We were taking things very slowly the past few months. Only seeing each other once a week, if that. Now we are up to twice a week, so it's a bit of an improvement. We didn't want to dive right into anything, especially after the heartbreak I put Hayden through."

I nodded, holding the top of the dress up in my hands as she continued to button. "You mean, after you literally ran away from him?"

"Yeah, I'd prefer not to relive that brief act of insanity," she looked down at the floor for a moment, her eyes threatening to tear. I wondered if any part of her still had feelings for Hayden. Or if she possibly loved him and just couldn't admit it to herself. I put a hand on her shoulder and she shook her head while offering me a small laugh. She smoothed out her black, cable-knit sweater and held her head up higher. "Anyway, won't you be twenty-six by the time you tie the knot? That's not too young. Plenty of people get married when they're even younger than that. Just not here in New York."

"I guess not," I shrugged. "I wonder what it's like out there in the real world." I tried to imagine getting married in my home town in Rhode Island, and how different it would be. I would most likely be having an outdoor wedding, not in a five-star hotel.

"You mean outside of New York?" she raised an eyebrow.

"Yeah," I played with my hair, twisting it around in my fingers. "I'll bet it's so much easier."

"What's easier?" she chuckled while cocking her head to the side.

"Everything," I mumbled. I let go of my hair and let out a sigh. "It's too bad I love living here too much to ever find out. I wouldn't even consider applying for doctoral programs outside of a thirty-mile radius."

Amalia nodded and then diverted her eyes to the ceiling. She offered me a small smile. I could tell she wanted me to be happier. I was standing in a bridal boutique surrounded by champagne and wedding gowns. But my mother's presence weighed on me too much to truly enjoy the moment.

"But back to Michael," she began with a heavy breath. "More than enough time has passed and he and I are ready to give this a real shot. Which means our first nice dinner together tonight at Café Grazie," I could hear the smile in her voice without even turning around. "Now I just have to figure out what to wear."

The more I thought about the idea of her and Michael dating, the more I disliked it. I knew I had to be a good friend and keep my mouth shut. Especially if I wanted her to continue helping me with my wedding-planning. Coyly, I kept the conversation about him going to hide my disdain.

"Oh, well maybe we can find you something here! I'm envisioning something in the magenta family," I shot her a look.

"That's a great idea!" she answered, with mock enthusiasm. "But no tacky bridesmaid dress. I'm going to go all-out! When he shows up, I'll just open the door to my apartment in a wedding gown." She cleared her throat and then starting talking in a robotic voice. "Michael, marry me. Beep."

"And then I will officially know two people who have literally run away from their significant other," I shook my head.

"Three if you count yourself, Miss NYU alumni mixer."

"Wow, you're right," I twisted my neck around to look at her. "What's wrong with us?"

"Living in New York City has ensorcelled us into becoming detached automatons all the while sundering us from the life we used to live. In short, we no longer act like normal people," she uttered flatly.

"Amen to that." I could feel Amalia on my back, struggling with each button. I made a mental note to leave a lot of extra time to put on this dress on the day of the wedding. She was taking forever and I was getting anxious. There were no mirrors in the dressing room, so I had no idea how I looked until I was able to step outside.

"Finished!" Amalia announced. "Turn around. Let me get a look at you."

I slowly turned around and let out a sound that sounded somewhere between a sigh and a laugh. "So?" I smoothed the dress down over my legs, "How does it look?"

"Immaculate," she said softly. "Alex is going to love it." She pulled me in for a hug and whispered in my ear, "Olivia, listen to me. Don't let your mother ruin this for you. You only get to do this once. If you're lucky, at least." She backed away, still holding onto my shoulders, and smiled warmly.

I felt tears threaten to pour out behind my eyes. She really was a great friend and here I was bashing the guy she liked, in my mind.

"Okay, missy. Now let's get out there so you can see how incredible you look."

The gown's train was short enough that I didn't need her to hold it behind me. I made my way out of the dressing room and walked into the main room with the podium. I carefully slid on the two-inch heels I had brought with me, to get an idea of how the dress would look with my wedding shoes on, and the nice brunette sales associate, whose name-tag read Jenna, offered me a veil. It was elegant with just a touch of lace. No glitter of any kind. I bent down so she could fasten it to my hair.

I took a deep breath and finally turned around to face the mirrors. I hardly recognized myself as I brought my hands to cover my mouth. The whiteness of the sheer veil created a deep contrast with my brown hair. The dress fit like a dream. Apart from the length, it would hardly need any alteration at all. My eyes welled with tears and I allowed myself to envision walking down the aisle, holding a bouquet of deep- pink peonies, my father on my arm, as I slowly made my way to Alex, who always looked amazing.

I gently held onto the bottom of my dress and turned to face

13

my mother, who was looking at me disapprovingly. I braced myself for what she was about to say. "What do you think, Mom?" I asked in a small voice.

She stood up and took a step back, taking the dress in. "Honestly? I think it's a bit bland, Olivia." My mother grimaced, her green eyes glazing over in a look that resembled sheer boredom.

"I happen to think that it's lovely," Amalia shot back at her. I pushed out a heavy breath. Leave it to Amalia to always speak her mind, no matter who was on the receiving end of it. I grinned widely and raised my eyes brows in triumph. Turning back to the mirror I stood up a little straighter, remembering Amalia's words in the dressing room. This dress was the one, just like Alex was the one. It was settled. This was the gown I was getting.

"Alright, then," I called over my shoulder to Jenna. "I'll have this one"

A few moments later, three other sales associates came darting over with small bells and began ringing them. A few of the other patrons in the store began to clap and I couldn't stop my face from turning at least three different shades of red. Amalia and I were instantly handed flutes of champagne, which we promptly clinked together. I took a small sip, careful not to spill any on the dress.

"To my friend, Olivia," Amalia cheered loudly. I laughed nervously and she grabbed my hand and pulled it up as I received the applause. To be fair, the associates were probably happier that I was spending two thousand dollars in their store than the fact that I had found the dress of my dreams.

I looked over to my mother one last time. Her attention was currently being held by her cell phone. I felt a pang of sadness. Even with all of the support around me, not having my mother's approval was painful. I shook my head and took another sip of my champagne, trying to ignore her callousness. She looked up at me one last time, a strange look in her eye.

For a moment there, it felt like pity.

Amalia turned to me and gave me a tight-lipped look that conveyed she had to leave.

"Go!" I laughed. "Have fun on your date with Michael and I'll see you on Monday."

Amalia rolled her eyes. "Right, for work-study with *Dr. Pain In the Ass*." She scratched her head.

"We have summer in a week," I offered. "It's already the last week of May."

"Don't you know?" she scrunched her face. "I'm working for him all summer," she grunted, while synchronously rolling her blue eyes. She always did have a flare for dramatics. "I don't have much of a choice. I really need the money. Oh well."

I offered her a small sympathetic smile and she made a beeline for the door. Even through the annoyance of having to work with Dr. Greenfield, her spirits were still high because of Michael. I wanted to be happy for her, but if it was up to me, I would have preferred her to continue seeing Hayden.

I turned and gave my dress a final once-over. It really was gorgeous, just like my fiancé. I couldn't ask for more. Screw everyone else! I was marrying the love of my life. Now I just needed to set a date.

Three – Amalia

As I pulled my jacket tighter around my chest on this particularly chilly May evening, I had a thought. Dating in New York City is not like dating in the rest of America. Or at least, how I imagine it is from the movies and television shows I've watched. If you live in, say, Virginia, and you are going on a date with a guy, he will most likely drive to your house, ring your door bell, and then walk you to his car, where he will open the passenger door for you and tell you how pretty you look. You'll smile as he closes the door, careful not to accidentally hit you with it, and you use the two seconds that it takes him to walk from one side of the car to the other to subtly run your fingers over your hair, because, *man*, that walk down the driveway really could have messed it up. Then the two of you will drive off to your destination, most likely The Cheesecake Factory, chatting the whole way there about what kind of music you like to listen to while you drive, and whether or not you still use your GPS to get to the mall.

When you live in Manhattan it's a little different. For one, no one is picking you up. Unless you live right near each other, which almost never happens, in which case you'll do one of the following together, you are responsible for your own transportation to and from the location that he most likely chose. So what are your choices? There are really only three options. Unless you have a lot of money to spend on a private car (such as an Uber cab), you are either walking, taking a cab, or taking the subway. All of these choices almost guarantee that you will look nothing like how you did when you left your apartment for this date. If you went down into the grody abyss that is the subway, your make-up has most likely melted off and been replaced with soot. There is no avoiding this. Even if you are only taking the train for one stop, you will be dirty when you exit the station. Another choice is walking. This can be nice if your date falls on one of the five days out of the whole year when the weather is bearable and you have on very comfortable shoes. But, you're going on a date, so why would you be wearing comfortable shoes? So the safest choice is probably to take a cab. Just make sure to account for the copious amounts of traffic in the city. For me, my date was at seven o'clock. Coming from Murray Hill I decided to give myself forty-five minutes to get to the Upper East Side to meet Michael for our dinner at Café Grazie.

I sat in the cab for exactly thirty minutes and made it to my destination with fifteen to spare. Now here's my trick. After being a gross cab for half an hour, I got on my phone and tried to find the closest Sephora to refresh myself before meeting with my date. You figure it's been over an hour since I last so much as looked in a mirror, so I need to use these fifteen minutes wisely.

As I follow the map on my phone to the store, a text from Michael comes in. I feel a rush of excitement as I click on the message icon.

On my way ;-)

That was all he wrote, but it was enough for my heart to skip a beat. Olivia was right. This was a big deal. Anything Michael and I had ever done before was in secret. Now we were going out to dinner on a bona fide date. I felt a fresh batch of nerves hit me as I entered the store and caught sight of myself in a mirror.

Damn it, New York, why are you so dirty?

I spent exactly ten minutes in there, applying some vanilla-scented cream to my hands, which were dryer than a mouth of sand from ever-present New York wind. Sad to say it, but it still felt like winter to me in April. I then made my way over to the make-up section, where I unashamedly swept a generous amount of forty-dollar blush on my cheekbones. While utilizing the mirror, I ran my fingers through my curls, trying to get them to resemble something less Bride of Frankenstein and more Carrie Bradshaw. I scanned the store, deliberately avoiding eye contact with anyone who worked there, and found the perfume wall. Now for the final touch. I picked up a Marc Jacobs perfume that I had been mulling over buying for some time now, and spritzed a small amount on my wrists.

I breathed a sigh of relief and turned on my heel to leave the store. That's when I saw her.

Cassandra.

The two of us hadn't spoken since Olivia's engagement party nearly six months ago. I watched as she gingerly made her way around the lip-gloss section, picking up two very similar shades of pink and studying them in the light. I wanted to go over to her and say something. I hated that we weren't speaking. I wanted to tell her I was going on a date with Michael. That I was a mental case who ran away from Hayden. I wanted to tell her about what a bitch Olivia's mom was being, and how overwhelmed I was with school. And I wanted to know all about what was going on with her too. Who was she dating? How was work going for her? Did she miss me?

I took a step forward and then I stopped myself. I had a tiny fantasy play out in my mind. One where I walk over to her, and she greets me with the same cold indifference she had for the better part of last year. I felt a pang of humiliation just thinking about it, and I had waited too long for a real shot with Michael to let anything put me in a sour mood tonight.

So I did what I had to do. I glided sideways out of the store and walked back the two blocks to the restaurant, where Michael was already waiting for me.

"I'll have the steak, medium rare," Michael uttered, squinting at the drinks menu. "And an old-fashioned." He subtly chewed on his bottom lip, momentarily distracting me.

The waitress smiled at him, her blue eyes lingering on him a little longer than necessary. They caught eyes as he handed her his menu, and he gave her a polite smile. I felt an instant pang of jealousy.

I smoothed my skirt out, careful not to accidentally hit my tights with a fingernail, and cleared my throat in an attempt to get the pretty waitress's attention. She turned her gaze to me and offered me a fake smile. "And for you, miss?"

"Penne in vodka sauce, with a side of steamed spinach," I beamed back. She could stare at him all she wanted. The fact was, he was out on a date with *me*. "And I'll also have a glass of cabernet. Thank you." I held out my menu with a triumphant smirk.

The waitress collected our menus and darted off to put our orders in. The restaurant was crowded, not unusual for a Saturday night. Michael caught eyes with me and I immediately melted. I wondered if he could hear my breathing get heavier whenever he was around. His dark hair was perfectly in place, and I wondered if he had gotten a haircut just for our date. He reached across the table for my hand, and I slowly slid mine over to his, scared that if I moved too quickly he'd pull it away in jest.

But he didn't pull away. He held my hand gently as we sat in a comfortable silence for a moment, gently easing into casual conversation.

"How was the wedding-gown search?" he asked, as the waitress dropped off our drinks. "Did Olivia find the dress of her dreams?"

"She did," I uttered through a wide smile. I must have looked like such a fool, but I didn't care. Even being here, now, across the table from Michael as he held my hand and asked me about my day, felt so surreal. Like any moment my alarm clock would go off and I'd wake up to find out that this was all just a cruel dream. That he had gotten back together with his ex-girlfriend, Marge, and I had broken things off with Hayden for nothing.

"What does it look like?" he asked, now smiling himself. For our first official date, Michael looked as extraordinary as ever, donning a dark-blue button-down, grey dress slacks, and black patent-leather shoes. I tried to hide a hard swallow as I thought about us going back to his apartment to be alone when dinner was over. I shook my head to clear my thoughts and tried to focus on the question he had asked me.

"What? I'm not telling you what her dress looks like!" I laughed, and then paused to sip my wine.

Michael's index finger drew small circles over my open palm on the table. Damn it, I'd give away government secrets if he kept that up!

"Why won't you tell me?" he asked, finally letting go of my grasp to take a sip of his drink. I felt a little disappointed that the touching had stopped.

"Because then you'll tell Alex and he'll know what his bride's wedding gown looks like," I raised my eyebrows.

"That's right, babe. Alex and I sit around gossiping about wedding gowns," he smirked. "Actually tomorrow he and I have plans to sit down and really bang out the roses-versus-peonies debate."

I blinked a few a times before answering him. "Did you just call me babe?"

"Penne Vodka?" the waitress plopped the bowl down in front of me, the sauce nearly spilling on my blouse. She carefully set Michael's food down in front of him, once again grinning like a mental patient. This time I ignored her staring and dug straight into my pasta. She walked away, strutting just a bit. Michael didn't look at her again.

"Question," I said to Michael, without looking up.

"Answer," he replied, while cutting his steak.

"Will you be my date to their wedding?" I held my breath the moment the words escaped my lips.

He looked up at me just as he was about to take a bite of his food. I sat for a moment, perfectly still as I awaited his response. It was kind of a hard question to answer, considering Olivia and Alex hadn't even set a date yet.

He offered me a small smile and said, "Sure."

I slowly let out my breath as he went back to eating.

Four – Olivia

Another summer came and went in New York City. I could swear they all felt the same. The weekends included walks in Central Park, iced lattes at cafés, and lots of people jogging down the waterfront in Battery Park. This summer was no different. While Amalia worked for Dr. Greenfield all summer long, I feverishly flipped through any wedding magazine I could get my hands on. I also spent a couple of weekends up in Rhode Island visiting my dad. The first time I arrived, he gleefully showed me the engagement announcement in the local newspaper that he had submitted on my behalf. He had copied a picture of Alex and myself from my Facebook page and submitted it along with a small description of us. It wasn't the picture I would have chosen, but it got the job done. It was so sweet of my dad to do that. My mother, on the other hand, continued her reign of terror while trying to micro-manage every detail of my wedding, for which I had yet to set a date. It was getting a little ridiculous, at this point, not having the date set, but Alex and I were so busy traveling back and forth to Rhode Island, and checking out doctoral programs to apply for, that we honestly hadn't had the time to scope out any venues.

Before I knew it, it was August and school was starting back. The best part of the summer was not having to work for Dr. Greenfield, but Monday morning that would all change. Monday marked the beginning of the end of graduate school. The first day of our final year. All of our doctoral program applications had to be in by February. It seemed a long time away, but I knew the time would fly by. Years seemed to be getting shorter with each passing birthday.

By Thursday morning, I was already in a routine. I was sat at one of the laptops Dr. Greenfield had set up for us in a small computer lab. The room was bleak and depressing. As I worked with the analysis program on the computer that was already making my head spin just ten minutes into me working on it, I knew I had to make a good impression on Dr. Greenfield if I wanted a letter of recommendation to the doctoral programs I would be applying to. I checked the clock on the screen – nine forty-five. Amalia was already fifteen minutes late and I could tell it would easily turn into a theme with her. I rubbed my eyes and tried to concentrate on the work in front of me. With all of the wedding ideas bouncing around my head, concentrating on this work-study program was getting harder and harder to do. At the computer next to me sat August Marek, Dr. Greenfield's little pet, with his head down and completely engrossed in the work in front of him. He was the final student picked for Dr. Greenfield's study, and his grades completely put mine to shame. He had managed to get an A in nearly all of his classes his entire time at NYU, and his key-chain told me he went to Brown for undergrad. I knew we weren't officially competing against each other, but being a woman already gave me a disadvantage just because there were so many women in the program. If he and I were going to apply for any of the same doctoral programs, the admissions office would choose him over me in a heartbeat.

A moment later, Amalia came bursting through the door, her purse falling off her shoulder as the door shut loudly behind her. She was wearing her typical jeans and sneakers, but looked a little classier than usual with a cream-colored sweater with rhinestone details around the collar. She had a small, Coach purse on her right shoulder and a take-away cup of coffee in her left hand. Dr. Greenfield and I looked up at her disturbance. Unflappable, August never took his eyes off the computer screen. Amalia opened her mouth to speak, but I shot her a look and then motioned to the empty chair next to mine.

"Miss Hastings," Dr. Greenfield said in a tight voice. "What did I tell you over the summer about showing up late for work?" His facial expression was a frightening one. For a brief moment I wondered what it would have been like to grow up in a household with that kind of man for a father. So strict and unrelenting.

"I'm really sorry, professor," she scrambled to get to her seat and turn her computer on. "I was coming from midtown, and the R train was running late." She placed the coffee down on the desk and I held my breath as I imagined her knocking it over. Thankfully she didn't.

Dr. Greenfield raised a hand, indicating her to stop speaking. "I'm not interested in your excuses. You either get here in time from here on out, or I will find someone else to take your position. Remember what I said last year? Don't make me fire you." He shook his head in disapproval. "We are as busy as a cat on a hot tin roof over here."

Amalia pursed her lips and August actually raised a puzzled eyebrow at Dr. Greenfield's remark. It was like our professor spoke another language than us. Sometimes it was comical, but I was in no mood today.

"It won't happen again," she muttered with wide eyes, and then immediately put her head down. She started fidgeting with her curls and I could tell she was embarrassed. I couldn't blame her, the professor was definitely nothing if not intimidating. Especially with his stern, booming southern accent.

Out of the corner of my eye, I could see the hint of a smile tug at August's lips. He knew he was Greenfield's favorite. August had taken classes from him before and apparently always aced every exam. I was really starting to dislike this guy. I narrowed my eyes at him, but he either didn't notice or didn't care.

Greenfield's eyes followed Amalia as she slowly lowered herself into the chair next to mine. Dr. Greenfield shook his head and returned to his books. Amalia let out a soft sigh.

"What are you working on?" she asked in a near-whisper, dropping her purse to the floor.

"Analyzing the data we collected on Monday," I replied. I touched my fingertips to my temple, feeling a dull headache coming on. "There's a lot of it."

"Just tell me how I can help," she offered me a weak smile. She looked past me for a moment. "Hey, August."

"Hey," he replied, without looking up. He let out a soft, exasperated sigh and pushed his sleeves up.

She rolled her eyes and I couldn't help but smile. I reached over to the empty desk across from me and grabbed a bunch of files with last Friday's date on them.

"Here," I handed them to her. "Start helping before you get fired and have to live on my and Alex's couch for the rest of the year."

"Stop threatening me with homelessness," she half-smiled. She flipped open the files and began to carefully type the data into the computer. "Speaking of you and Alex, are you going to move out of your apartment? Or is he going to move out of his?"

"We haven't decided yet, but clearly his building is a lot nicer than mine. I'd much rather live there. I will miss living in Brooklyn, though, Roosevelt Island is a much different change of scenery," I offered in a near-whisper.

"Well, I won't miss you living in Brooklyn," she gave me an over-the-top smile. "But back to you, I highly doubt he'd say no to you living with him. From the one time I was over there, it seemed to me like he really loved his place. Plus, guys hate moving."

"Everyone hates moving," I let out a soft chuckle. "I just hope he doesn't hate having to make room for all of my stuff!" I rubbed my temples, suddenly overwhelmed by the professor's research project, my regular classes, moving, and planning a wedding all within a little over a year. I took a deep breath and shook my head. "But you're right, I'll talk to him about it after we book a venue for the wedding." I suddenly felt a strong urge to change the subject. "Can you grab lunch later this week so I can hear about your first official date with Mr. Big, I mean Michael?"

She nodded quickly, but then immediately turned the conversation back to me. "Have you narrowed it down at all?" she looked up from her screen.

"Narrowed what down?" I asked, suddenly feeling warm. I pulled at the collar on my shirt for extra breathing room.

Amalia shook her head in surprise. "Your venue, of course. As your maid of honor it's my job to remind you that these places book up very far in advance, and it's already the end of August!"

August shot his head up and glared at us.

"Not you," Amalia waved him off. The *month*."

He grimaced and robotically returned to his work.

Without missing a beat, she continued. "Have you thought about wanting your wedding in a hotel or maybe something outside of the city by a lake somewhere?" She looked up at the ceiling and then made a face at what I assumed was having to go to some random sleepy-town she had never heard of. She was never one for the outdoors. She turned her eyes back to me and plainly asked, "Do you even know what season you want to get married in?"

Before I could respond, August lifted his head again and shot us a look, his dark-blue eyes flashing with annoyance. Even though his eyes were also blue, they were a big contrast to Amalia's, which were always wide and youthful. August's reminded me of a villain in a super-hero movie.

Amalia met his gaze and held it. For a moment, it was if they were having some adolescent staring contest. I glanced back at the professor again, who wasn't paying attention to us. I looked a little more closely at him and noticed his eyes were fixed on a wooden picture frame in the corner of his desk. I never noticed the frame before, but then again I had never really looked that hard at his desk. He must have felt my eyes fixed on him because he looked up and frowned.

I cleared my throat and excused myself. Grabbing my cell phone, I headed out into the hallway and walked out of earshot. My mind spinning in a thousand different directions, I grabbed a seat on one of the small benches in the hall. Remembering Alex didn't have class until later this afternoon, I hit the speed-dial and waited for him to pick up. He picked up on the second ring. I could hear the bustle of the city in the background.

"Hey, babe," I pushed out in a breathy voice. "Are you busy right now?"

"Just got off the train to meet Michael for a cup of coffee, but I have a little bit before then. Is everything alright?"

Everything most certainly was not alright, but where did I begin? I decided to start with something that Alex could actually help me with.

"I am feeling overwhelmed with the wedding planning," I confessed, feeling my shoulders sink.

"What's overwhelming about it?" he asked. "We haven't even started yet."

"That's why I'm overwhelmed," I explained. "It's getting kind of late in the game. I think this weekend we should start looking at venues, maybe we can start with a few downtown places like the Mondrian Hotel in SoHo and Bridgewaters in the South Street Seaport? And maybe we can finalize the decision of whether or not we want to wait until after graduation to get married?"

"Absolutely, baby," he said calmly, and I immediately felt better for having called him. "But unfortunately I think Bridgewaters may have closed."

"That was kind of my first choice," I sighed. I pulled a piece of my brown hair up to my eyes and studied it. I had better get it cut now so I didn't have to get another haircut before the wedding.

"Okay, I'll make a few calls and have some venues lined up for us this weekend."

"It *is* going to be okay, sweetheart. And just know this; I cannot wait to marry you."

As soon as he said that, I felt a warm rush throughout me. As stressful as it was, this wasn't going to be like last year. I wasn't going to freak out and push him away.

"I can't wait to marry you either," I uttered. I felt a warm rush dance around my chest. "I love you. Thank you for talking to me."

Alex laughed. "You don't ever have to thank me for talking to you!"

I checked the clock on the wall and peeled myself off the bench. "I had better get in there before Dr. Greenfield fires me."

"He's not going to fire you," Alex replied in a sing-song tone. "But, yes, get back to work and I'll see you tonight. You can tell me all about how the study is going."

"Do I have to?" I teased.

"Bye, darling," he laughed.

I hung up the phone and smiled. Thank goodness for Alex. I made a mental note that after we'd picked a wedding venue, we really needed to sit down and decide which doctoral programs we'd be applying to. I let out another sigh and tucked my cell into my back pocket.

As soon as I let go of it, my phone started vibrating. I grunted while quickly checking to see who it was. I had to look at the phone twice just to make sure I was reading it correctly. It was a text from my mother, who has never texted in her life.

She wrote, "Olivia, we need to talk in person. Meet me at the King Cole Bar at six o'clock."

You have got to be kidding me. Why would I haul all of the way uptown just to talk to her when she'd been an absentee parent for years? Shaking my head, I took a few more steps closer to the computer lab. A moment later my phone buzzed again. This time, she had my full attention.

"It's important, Olivia. It's about Alex."

Five – Amalia

On Thursday, I finally had a day off from Dr. Greenfield's lab, but unfortunately it didn't mean I had a day off from class. When the spring semester started back up last February, it became clear that getting the classes you wanted was nearly impossible. Now that we were in our final year, we didn't get to choose *anything*.

Thankfully, working in the research lab counted as a course, which meant I was only taking two classes this semester, Family Studies on Tuesdays and Gender and Contemporary Issues. Gender and Contemporary Issues was today at one o'clock and lasted until three o'clock. Although I wasn't thrilled with the required courses I had to take, this was the first time at NYU that I didn't have class either first thing in the morning or at six o'clock at night.

I finished packing my bag and headed into my bathroom to spruce myself up a bit, saying a silent thank you every time I remembered what it was like to have two roommates. I *really* loved living alone.

I was meeting Olivia for lunch at twelve, and then we were going straight to class together. Michael was also in this class, so I needed to look good. Even after knowing him for two years, I still got nervous every time I was around him.

Class with Michael was sometimes a little awkward. We didn't always sit directly next to each other, although we always sat in the same row with Olivia and Alex. I couldn't pinpoint what exactly caused my discomfort, but I couldn't help but compare myself to Olivia and Alex. They always looked like a couple. Even when they were sitting together in complete silence, there was this undeniable connection between the two of them. I wondered what people thought when they saw Michael and me sitting together. Or if they even noticed at all.

I swept the final coat of mascara over my lashes and rifled through my closet until I found a new lightweight jacket I had just bought from a boutique in the Village. I didn't make a ton of money working at the school, but I made enough to buy something for myself every once in a while. I pulled off the tags and slipped my arms through the tan-colored coat sleeves. Grabbing my iPod, I dashed to the door and slammed it shut behind me.

As I was walked toward the subway terminal, I felt my cell phone vibrate through my purse. I decided I had better check it in case it was Olivia cancelling our plans. But it wasn't from Olivia: it was from Hayden. My heart fell into my stomach and I begin to read the message.

"Hey, Amalia. I just wanted to see how you were. It's been a while since I last spoke to you. I was hoping we could get together for a drink. Maybe we could try to be friends? Let me know when you're available."

I stood at the top of the subway terminal re-reading the message. A group of men on their way to work loudly cleared their throats behind me to get through. "Sorry," I mumbled, stepping aside to let them pass. I had no idea how to respond, or if I even should. I shook my head and put my cell phone back in my purse, resolving to deal with Hayden's message later.

One subway ride later, I was at Artichoke, one of my favorite pizza places in the city. Unfortunately, most of my appetite had been destroyed by anxiety. Olivia was already standing outside of

31

the restaurant waiting for me, passively looking at something on her phone and smoking a cigarette.

"Is it just me, or is the subway becoming more disgusting with each passing day?" I muttered with a grimace. I didn't want to talk to Olivia about Hayden's message until I could fully process what it meant. Did I want to be friends with him? More importantly, why would he want to be friends with me after the way I treated him?

"It's even worse when you're coming from Brooklyn," she slipped her cell into the back pocket of her jeans and flicked the cigarette on the ground. She looked down at it for a second and pursed her lips.

She had a sullen look on her face and her eyes were glassy. But before I could open my mouth to ask her what was wrong she started back up.

"Maybe I should try to quit smoking before the wedding."

"Finally!" I shook my head. "Think of it as the first step towards saving up for your honeymoon."

She let out a chuckle but it sounded a bit broken. Something was definitely wrong.

The host showed us to our seats and we settled into a small booth. Before we could even place our drink orders, Olivia began to grill me about my and Michael's date.

"I asked him to be my date to your wedding," I smiled. I could feel myself blushing and reached for a glass of water. Thinking about Michael as my wedding date was an instant mood boost. He would easily be the most handsome guy there.

"You do know we haven't even set a date yet?" she replied in a mocking tone, without looking up from her menu.

"I know, and he still said yes!" I lightly tapped my hands on the table to get her attention.

"I'll have him usher you down the aisle," she offered, her gaze still on the menu. "Since he's going to be a groomsman. Oh, and Alex and I are going to look at some venues this weekend, so we should know a date soon enough."

For someone who was getting a dream wedding, she certainly didn't seem very happy about it. I wondered if she and Alex had gotten into some kind of squabble.

I twisted a curl around in my finger and let out a soft sigh. For a moment I let myself image would it would be like to have a wedding of my own, even though I was in no rush to get married. I let the fantasy dance around my head. I envisioned a small wedding on a beach somewhere like the Virgin Islands. I would be wearing a short, but elegant, wedding dress, with a bouquet of brightly colored flowers. Michael in a crisp, linen suit, looking more perfect than ever.

Apparently Olivia noticed me day-dreaming because the next thing I saw was her snapping her fingers in front of my face. "Earth to Amalia. We're splitting the pizza with the artichokes on it?" she cocked her head to the side.

"Obviously," I said in a mocking tone. "So back to my date, we went out to dinner and it was wonderful." I let out a dramatic sigh. I felt like a love-sick teenager and had no doubt in my mind that I was coming off as one too.

She seemed to consider this.

"What was the best part?" she leaned closer to me, her charm bracelets clanking on the table.

"Going back to his apartment and not feeling like I was doing anything wrong when I spent the night," I laughed nervously as I remembered the days of sneaking around. "And then having coffee with him in the morning before I left. I felt like we were a real couple."

"But you're not, are you?" she asked, looking me straight in the eyes. "I mean, you're not in a committed relationship."

"No, not yet," I swirled my straw around in my water glass. "But I'm sure it's just a matter of time." It bothered me that she had to point that out so declaratively.

"Are you still in love with him?" she continued, with wide eyes.

I chewed on my bottom lip. "I don't know if I ever really stopped being in love with him. Even when I was with Hayden, who I cared about *so* much, I never completely stopped thinking about Michael. It was as if my feelings for him were simply put on hold, like they were in remission, but never completely eradicated." I felt guilty for saying that after how wonderfully Hayden treated me. He had even told me he loved me, but I never felt sure enough about our relationship to say it back.

Olivia nodded and looked as if she was thinking this information over. "Does that mean you wouldn't hook up with anyone else? Even though the two of you are just dating?"

I quickly shook my head. I couldn't tell whether she was trying to drag me down into her bad mood or not, but her demeanor was definitely starting to get on my nerves.

"No," I leaned my chin on my palm of my hand and scrunched up my face at the thought of being with another guy. "I wouldn't want to do anything to jeopardize being with him."

"Do you think he would?" she asked, softening a bit.

I opened my mouth to answer, but then closed it. I just sat there for a moment, trying to form a sentence. The idea of Michael sleeping with someone else was extremely painful, even though we weren't in a committed relationship.

"I don't know," was all I could muster up. A wave of jealousy rolled through my chest and stomach at the idea of Michael even kissing another girl. I shook my head, telling myself not to think that way.

"I'm sorry," Olivia said flatly. "I didn't mean to upset you."

I wasn't sure why, but the question continued to bounce around in my mind. Would he continue to date other girls? Or were we trying to work toward something together?

"I'm alright," I lied, forcing a smile on my face. I ran my hands over my forehead and then through my hair. "What about you, Olivia? Are you alright?" I asked softly?

She just nodded and gave me a crooked smile.

"We should order because we're going to be late to class," I

34

closed my menu.

"Sure," she said, cocking her head to the side. I could tell what she was thinking, and what that look meant. Pity. And I hated being pitied.

The next morning I woke up early and decided to take an impromptu stroll at around eight-thirty over to the farmer's market set up in Union Square. Being that the Union Square subway entrance was one of the easiest ways to transfer to any line in the city, the neighborhood was always busy. This morning, however, 14th street was downright packed. I thought about turning back for a moment, but then I remembered the contents of my refrigerator were low, and I could really use some fresh fruit.

As I browsed a stand boasting the best apples in the city, I got a funny feeling. Like someone was watching me. I paid the cashier for a few apples and then turned around to see if I was going crazy. I wasn't. Two stands over, next to a woman selling artisan jam, stood Cassandra. She was mulling over a purchase as she looked up and caught my eye. I froze. This was the second time I had seen her out in the wild. I still had no intention of walking over to her. The last thing I said to her was that she owed me an apology. I'm still waiting for one.

We both just stood there for a moment, watching each other. It was obvious she was on her way to work. She was wearing a light-blue, knee-length dress with nude pumps. I had donned sweat pants and an old David Bowie t-shirt. I felt a pang of sadness as I remembered how close we were just a little over a year ago. I missed her. As I watched her gaze leave mine, her hand reach into her purse, and hand the woman cash in exchange for the jam, it dawned on me that she really didn't miss me. She didn't look back at me after that, she just took off. I watched her strut to the corner of 13th and Broadway so she could more easily hail a cab to work.

I took a deep breath and a few warm tears hit my cheeks. I didn't know what to think. How could someone change so much in such a short amount of time? And then I thought of my ex-boyfriend, Nicholas. Hadn't something similar happened to him? I wiped the tears away, but they just kept coming. Was something in the water here? How was it that two people who were such a huge part of my life, could just morph into completely different individuals and utterly not care if they ever saw or spoke to me again. Granted, I was the one who had broken things off with Nick the second time around. But that was after he turned into a power-hungry snob. I bit my bottom lip and wondered if the same thing was happening to Cassandra.

I finally stopped crying long enough to check the time on my phone. I had a "good morning" text from Michael that allowed my trembling lips to smile. I texted him back, popped on my headphones, and walked back to my neighborhood with my apples in tow.

Six – Olivia

"So what did you think of that last venue we looked at?" Alex crossed over to me from the kitchen. He plopped down on the sofa and started to untie his suede John Varvatos shoes. We had spent the entire day looking at venues.

I took a deep breath and started cracking my knuckles out of stress. We had just gotten off the train and walked all the way from the subway exit back to Alex's apartment. We were both beat.

The truth was, I loved the last place we looked at. The Mondrian Hotel down in SoHo offered a beautiful entryway with a garden-like atmosphere and French-style decorating all throughout the hotel. The downside? It was two hundred and fifty dollars a head for a Saturday wedding, and only a bit cheaper for a Friday night at two twenty five.

What Alex didn't know was that I had met my mother at the King Cole Bar the other day to talk about him. For the most part, I don't give much weight to my mother's opinions. But when she told me over a glass of wine that she "swore" she saw Alex out with another girl, I couldn't ignore it.

"I thought it was gorgeous," I said through a sigh, my mother's smug face popping into my mind. "Perfect in fact."

Alex straightened up on the couch and offered me a smile. "Then why do you look so sad, baby?"

The reason I looked so sad was clear. After I told my mother that she was wrong, that she couldn't have possibly seen something that was more than a friendly *hello* with a fellow classmate, she pulled out her phone and showed me a picture.

I couldn't see who the girl was, because she was facing the other way. From what I could tell she was wearing heels and had long, red hair. But what I could clearly see was Alex's face. The two of them were embraced in a hug and, from what I could tell, it was around our school.

"He's cheating on you," she had said, in between sips of her Bordeaux.

I shook my head at her. "You're wrong. I know there's an explanation."

But deep down I didn't know for sure that Alex wouldn't cheat on me. I believed anyone was capable of doing anything. And my mother planting seeds of doubt in my mind only made me feel worse. Taking the phone out of her hand, I texted the picture to my phone and told her I had to leave.

Now, with Alex still waiting for an answer as to why I looked so sad, I realized I wasn't ready to talk to him about it yet.

"Because this wedding is going to end up costing upwards of fifty grand by the time all is said and done." I immediately craved a cigarette. I instinctively reached for my pack in my purse, and then bit my bottom lip in frustration when I remembered that I was trying to quit and hadn't bought a new pack this morning. "And that's not including what our honeymoon is going to cost. At this point we'd be lucky to afford a motel at the Jersey shore."

Alex let out a chuckle and wrapped his strong arms around me. As soon as his body pressed onto mine, I felt myself relax. The truth was, I wanted a big wedding. I wanted the white dress, the long aisle to float down, the candles, the flowers, the band, and, most of all, to celebrate it with everyone I cared about. But at the end of the day, I would gladly trade all of those novelties for a small ceremony at an upstate bed and breakfast if it meant I got to be with Alex. I felt a small wave of insecurity as I wondered if he felt the same way. If he would be happy with that.

As long as that was still what *he* wanted.

I turned to face him, feeling the warmth of his comforting smile. We'd come a long way in these past two years. First our relationship had started out as a secret that only he and I knew about. Then, last year, I essentially freaked out and felt like I didn't know what I wanted. I was confused, but the truth was, deep in my heart of hearts, there's only one guy I ever truly loved. And that was my husband-to-be. I pushed the thoughts of him hugging some other girl into the back of my mind and reminded myself that Alex was a good person.

"Olivia," he picked up my left hand and softly kissed it. "We will set a budget for this wedding, and try as hard as we possibly can not to go over it. Don't worry about the honeymoon either. I already started saving money the moment you said yes to marrying me."

I looked at him with raised eyebrows.

Alex let out a soft chuckle. "Okay, I know what you're thinking. Trust-fund baby had to save money? Well, actually, yes. I was paying off my tuition for NYU as I went. I never took out student loans. But after I bought the engagement ring, I realized I was going to have to. So, yes, I will have a bit of debt from NYU when I graduate. But I will gladly spend the next twenty years paying it off if it means I get to marry you."

"Your debt would only be for our final year, right?" I asked. I was touched by Alex's sacrifice. He was already paying for most of the wedding himself. My father had generously offered to kick in about six thousand dollars, but two thousand of it had already gone to my dress, leaving us with just about enough money to pay a florist. I gave Alex a tight-lipped smile. It was a weird feeling, to have both appreciation and anxiety at the same time.

"Baby, thank you so much for taking on this financial burden," I uttered. "I feel very guilty about it, and wish I could do more. Honestly, guilt isn't even the word. Anxiety is." I felt my hands begin to shake. "I don't have any savings."

"Olivia, you have to calm down a bit. About the wedding, about school, about what doctoral program you're going to end up in when we graduate. All of it. Because if you don't, you're going to miss it."

"Miss what?" I asked, genuinely confused by his statement.

"Everything," he said with a straight face. Planning your wedding is supposed to be a happy and enjoyable time in your life. Sure, there are common stressors that every couple goes through. But I don't want you to look back five, or ten, years from now and wish you had appreciated it more. We're only going to get to do this once." He looked away for a moment and chewed on his bottom lip. "At least I only plan on doing this once."

That's when I realized what I was doing to Alex. My anxiety and obsession over everything working out perfectly was making him feel insecure. A fresh wave of guilt hit me and I immediately reached for his hands.

"I am doing this *once*," I said in a measured tone. "Only once. You are the person I want to marry and this is not cold feet, or doubts about you. And I am so sorry if it came across that way." I squeezed his hand a little tighter. "Till *death* do us part. Not divorce!"

"So, then let's go with the Mondrian!" he exclaimed. "I mean, it's gorgeous, it's in the city, the food is fantastic, and it's a hotel, so all of our out-of-town guests will have a place to stay. Also, they did have an opening on the day you wanted."

I bolted up from the couch and snatched my cell phone off the coffee table.

"What are you doing?" he widened his eyes. Probably the sexiest thing he did, without knowing it.

"I'm calling them," I said through an over-sized grin. "I'm done obsessing about this. You're right. They have the date we want, they have the space, they have everything. I am calling them right now and booking our wedding for July of next year. One month

40

after graduation and at least a month before we have to start any doctoral programs. It's going to be wonderful."

Alex stood up next to me and leaned in for a soft, buttery kiss. I stood up on my toes to reach him and he bent down slightly to lift me up. He held me in his arms for a moment and then said, "Don't call them. I want to be the one to do it. Is that alright?"

I nodded and he loosened his grip and slowly lowered me down until my toes reached the hardwood floors. He kissed me on the forehead and then made a beeline for his cell phone, which was sitting on the counter top in the kitchen. Phone still in hand, I scrolled through my contacts until I found Amalia's number and started to compose a text message.

Hey, Maid-of-Honor! Not sure what your plans are for after graduation. Hopefully you're not planning on taking off to Abu Dhabi, or something, because I need you here in June.

Save the date, girl. I'm getting married Saturday, July 15th!

Seven – Amalia

What does one wear to a fancy, black-tie wedding in downtown Manhattan? I touched my finger to my lips as I scanned the fridge for a bottle of water. This would be a perfect job for Cassandra.

I found the bottle and closed the fridge door. It didn't matter, Cassie wouldn't be at Olivia's wedding and it was still far enough away for me not to need to worry about finding the perfect dress. Come to think of it, Olivia would probably have my dress picked out for me since I was in the wedding party.

A few days after Olivia texted me that she was getting married July 15th, I received an email from Dr. Greenfield summoning me to his office. He said he had something important to talk to me about, and it couldn't wait until the next time I was due to report to work-study.

I got to his office around nine-thirty, trying to look as put together as possible with grey dress pants and a burgundy blouse on top. I even pulled my usually untamable curls into a low ponytail. Everyone at my school always seemed so dressed-up, so put together. I thought back to the first time I met Michael, how his demeanor and confidence had completely tripped me up for the rest of my day. No matter what I wore, or how put-together I pretended to be, I always felt dowdy next to the rest of my classmates. And that went double for the professors. But

Dr. Greenfield didn't seem to pay any attention to my outfit as he motioned for me to take a seat on the oversized leather chair across from his mahogany desk. As I lowered myself into the chair, I noticed a picture frame face down next to a stapler on his desk. I thought it was weird, but then again, I thought everything about the professor was a little off.

"Amalia," he began, folding his hands in front of him and leaning just a bit forward. "As you know, NYU offers a few different work-study programs to its students to help them make extra money while they're enrolled here."

I nodded my head, never taking my eyes off him. I was determined to remain calm and collected. I wouldn't interrupt or let my gaze drift over. This way he couldn't perceive anything I did to be rude.

Every time this man spoke to me, I felt small and insubstantial. Whenever I sat through one of his classes or so much as took a meeting with him, I wanted to be anywhere but there. I think, on some level, it played into the idea that maybe I just really never belonged here at this school.

"Beginning this fall, the doctoral students in the psychology department here at NYU will have the opportunity to partake in the counseling program for work-study. Only a select few will be chosen, the best and the brightest, of course." He rung his hands together and smirked. "We wouldn't want anyone in there talking to the younger cohort if they didn't know what they were doing."

I cocked my head to the side and opened my mouth just a bit, but then quickly closed it. I wanted to make sure I phrased, *what the heck are you talking about?* in the most respectful way possible.

"Sir," I said, crossing my right leg over my left. "I'm not exactly sure what this has to do with me."

Dr. Greenfield had a frustrated look on his face. "As part of their requirement to graduate, the psychology students have to conduct psychoanalysis on individuals to prove they have a great enough understanding of the knowledge they've obtained while they have been studying here. There are a few ways to get volunteers for this treatment." He stood up and slowly began pacing the room. His steps were small for a man of his height, and he kept his head down the entire time. I began to wonder if something was bothering him, but didn't dare ask.

"Treatment?" I whispered the word, unsure of what he was getting at.

"It's really a win-win situation," he stopped pacing and looked at me. "You would come in twice a week for about forty-five minutes a session, and one of the senior-level doctoral students would analyze you. They would get the credit and experience they need, plus a little extra money, and you would get free analysis."

Without noticing, I shot up from the chair. "I don't need analysis. I'm not crazy." I immediately sat back down and folded my hands in my lap. So much for coming across as professional or not seeming crazy.

Dr. Greenfield shook his head. I could almost hear him mentally wish he had a glass of scotch at that very moment. "Just the fact that you think analysis is only for the clinical population proves how far behind you are here, Amalia." His eyes were narrowed and he had an undeniable look of disappointment on his face. I lowered my head in embarrassment. Shame crept through me like the kind of goose bumps you'd get when you had a fever. I didn't know which was worse, the fact that I had been recommended for psychological treatment by my professor, or that said professor just confirmed my fears that I wasn't doing well in the program.

"This isn't something I feel comfortable with," I said, shrugging, reaching my arms around my stomach, this conversation suddenly feeling vexatious, "I am afraid I'm going to have to decline."

"That's a shame, Ms. Hastings," his voice was low and wry. But I should tell you, if you don't partake in this portion of the work-study program, then you can no longer work on my project with me." I saw a small smile tug at the side of his lips, or maybe I was imagining that.

"Excuse me?" I uttered, trying to keep an even tone. "Since when did going to analysis become a requirement for working on your project?" I had read the forms thoroughly before signing – at least I thought I had.

"You've shown me how irresponsible you can be, and how little effort you are willing to put in to further your education, and ultimately, your career. I asked you this a while ago, Miss Hastings, and you didn't have a good answer for me then and I doubt you have a good answer for me now. What do you want to do when you graduate with your Master's from NYU?"

I was speechless. The truth was, with everything going on in my life over the past few years, just handling things day to day felt like a constant struggle. The future seemed so far away when I first moved into that West Village apartment, but isn't that how it always goes? One day you're imaging your future, then in the blink of an eye, it's here.

But now, the cushy idea of "future Amalia" having to make these decisions was gone. The time was now. I only had a little over a year left here and I had to start making some serious plans for my future.

I looked down at the floor. The old, slightly torn, carpeting mirrored my feelings of uselessness. Maybe going to therapy wasn't such a bad idea after all.

Without further consideration, I backed down.

"You're right," I conceded.

"What was that?" he took a step closer to me and turned his head slightly as if to indicate that he wanted me to speak louder.

My feelings of dejection slowly melded into ones of anger. I felt my hands ball in fists. The man was getting way too much enjoyment out of this.

"I'll stay in your program," I enunciated each word through gritted teeth. "I need the money. So I guess that means, starting in the fall, I will be going to analysis."

"It will begin at the end of October."

I nodded, unsure of what else to say.

Dr. Greenfield stared at me for a moment. The wrinkles around his eyes looked more pronounced today than usual, and for a moment I felt sorry for him. What did I really know about this man? His arms were folded across his chest and I noticed he didn't wear a wedding ring. I let my shoulders sink a bit and relaxed. There was really no point in me getting all worked up about this. One more year in this hell hole, and I'd be out. Might as well make it as easy on myself as I could while I was here.

I took a deep breath. "Is that all, sir?" I kept my face poker-straight, unwilling to take any more criticism.

He looked at me for a beat longer and then said, "Yes, that's all."

I turned on my heel and headed toward the door, chewing on the bottom of my lip the whole time.

"Oh and Miss Hastings," he called out to me just as I was turning the doorknob. "When you get here Monday morning, do not be late again. This is your final warning."

I merely turned to him and nodded, unable to speak out of fear I would curse him out.

Eight – Olivia

Three months later

It was fall again in New York, which means you could expect to see lots of Burberry scarves, black tights, pumpkin spice lattes, and fingerless gloves. Here in the city, and in most of the northern states, fall lasts for about two weeks until the harsh, oppressive winter begins. It was September 14th and classes had been going on for nearly three weeks. Our cohort only had four classes left to finish our requirements for graduation. Two this semester and two in the spring. Of course, our senior seminar class was being taught by Dr. Greenfield. There was just no escaping that man. We could all at least take solace in the fact that senior seminar was a core class and was only held once a semester. We would all be taking it together. The other class that Alex and I chose this semester was called "Cell Biology – the Nucleus and Beyond." Alex pointed out that the class would stand out more on our doctoral applications than any of the other courses being held. I thought it sounded like a *Star Trek* episode and agreed to enroll.

Deep breath.

I sipped my green tea grabbed from a local café near Union Square and slowly walked to my biology class. I wanted to savor the beautiful weather while I could. It was a little after two-thirty and my building was about ten minutes away. I had plenty of time to make it to my three o'clock class. I took another deep breath as a pair of two teenage girls walked passed me, giggling as they scarfed down cupcakes from one of the artisan food trucks parked by the curb. They looked so happy and full of life. Even at twenty-four, a considerably young age, I felt deflated.

I hadn't spoken to my mother much since the day she told me about the picture. The picture of Alex hugging another girl. She had sent me a couple of follow-up texts asking me if I'd confronted him yet. I asked her in the politest way possible to butt out. Not because I necessarily wanted to be nice to her, more that I didn't want to engage with her in a conversation about nonsense.

I shook my head, putting thoughts of her out of my mind, and took a soothing sip of my tea. Eight more months and then we would graduate on May 17th. Graduation this year, like most years, was being held at Yankee Stadium, which is located in the Bronx. I would have preferred it been anywhere else. Preferably somewhere inside with air conditioning that wouldn't take me nearly an hour to get to from my and Alex's apartment on Roosevelt Island.

The summer hadn't helped to calm me down at all. While most people were sunning themselves in the Hamptons or on Fire Island, I was filling out applications and gathering letters of recommendations for the programs at NYU, Sarah Lawrence College, New School University, and Hunter College. In between all of that, I was constantly flipping through bridal magazines and meeting with vendors for the wedding. It was astonishing how far out in advance everything had to be booked. Not to mention I spent two weeks in August moving out of my apartment in Brooklyn and moving into Alex's place on Roosevelt Island.

I was mentally wrecked by everything that was going on. Even with the support I had from my father and from Alex, my mother's lack of positive interest in my wedding was really starting to take a toll. She was bent on getting me to break it off. I shouldn't be surprised; our relationship had always been strained. But for some reason, getting married really makes you realize who's truly there for you and who isn't. It is, arguably, the most important thing you will ever do in your life. If someone can't make the time for you while that's going on, they'll never be there for you.

On top of everything else, quitting smoking was a total bitch. I was constantly tempted to sneak a cigarette whenever Amalia wasn't looking.

My wedding was less than a year away, and I couldn't even enjoy being engaged because of all of my schoolwork. I thought about what Alex had said to me, that I'm missing it. I shook my head once more, trying to drown out the anxious thoughts that had planted roots in my mind.

I had to drop out of Greenfield's lab because there just wasn't enough time to get everything done. For now, at least, I didn't have to worry about paying rent. Since we were engaged, Alex's father had agreed to let me live in Alex's apartment and not pay rent. I was relieved for the time being, but after the wedding there was no way I was allowing Alex and me to be trapped under his father's thumb. No matter what, we had to find a way to pay for the apartment ourselves. Or move into a smaller place.

One thing was sure, neither one of us wanted to leave New York. And considering that all of the school's we were applying to were here, moving somewhere else wasn't even an option.

As I walked up to the building, a group of students was outside smoking. All other thoughts in my mind suddenly shut down and all I could think about was how badly I wanted to smoke. A chorus of nicotine-withdrawn voices flooded my head like a swarm of bees to a hive.

Ask them for a cigarette. You're so stressed out. One cigarette isn't going to hurt.

I pressed the palms of my hands to my eyes and could feel warm tears from stress building up behind them.

Just fucken do it. Who cares? Oh my God, let go and smoke. Smoke! Smoke! Smoke!

"Oh my God," I uttered. I stood perfectly still, afraid if I moved even an inch, my body would shatter from pressure.

"Olivia?" a soft voice came from behind me.

Startled, I wiped my eyes quickly and dropped my hands to my sides. They made a slapping sound as they hit my jeans.

"Babe?" Alex asked, concern in his eyes. "Are you alright?"

I gave him the best smile I could muster up. "Cigarette craving," I shrugged, leaving out the other half of my internal meltdown.

Alex gave me a sympathetic grimace. "I know *exactly* how you feel."

"Probably," I whispered, a cold breeze rustling through my hair.

"Come on," he reached for my hand. "Let's get to class. This nucleus isn't going to study itself."

"I don't even know how to respond to that," I laughed, as I took a step past the group of smokers who were extinguishing their respective cigarettes.

"I made you laugh, though," he pulled me in for a kiss. There was one strong advantage to us having quit smoking. Our kisses had never been better. For one, I never really noticed how Alex tasted before. Our mouths had always been coated, but now it was like our senses were coming back to us. Even his smell was stronger than ever. His cologne, his aftershave, his shampoo, I could smell it all as he softly pressed his body against mine and ran him fingers through my hair. This new high I got from kissing was better than smoking and after a few seconds my nicotine craving had vanished. I pulled away, flushed even though it was only fifty degrees outside.

"Let's go to class," I mumbled begrudgingly. I looked up at him through my lashes, my mind on other things.

He leaned down and kissed my forehead. "I love you," he whispered. "You love me, right?"

As we passed by more students and faculty members, something struck me as familiar.

A girl, with long red hair, talking to one of the professors. I scanned down her frame and noticed a pair of black high heels. I felt the color drain from my face, but immediately began fighting the doubt.

Washington Square Park is a very popular area of Manhattan. Lots of people, from all over New York, come here just to embrace its beauty. It doesn't mean that's the same girl from the picture.

It doesn't mean he's cheating on you.

"Of course I love you," I stood on my toes to reach his face. "To the moon and back."

Nine – Amalia

Heavy waves of rain hit the floor-to-ceiling windows of Michael's apartment, making the inside feel more of an aquarium than a home. I was sitting on his couch, scanning over the paper work for enrolling in the work-study analysis program. Michael stood over the stove, with his sleeves rolled up to show off his forearms. A part on the male body I also happened to like. He carefully sprinkled salt into his mixture, perfecting his mushroom risotto.

In true eleventh-hour fashion, I was filling out the new work-study papers that were due Monday. Monday was tomorrow. I rubbed my blurry eyes and resolved to get this finished tonight.

In case of emergency contact _____

I looked up at Michael for a moment and smiled, but wrote down Olivia Davis, including her phone number and new address with Alex.

"What are you doing over there?" Michel called over the sounds of the stove-top fan. Lightning struck and illuminated the entire apartment.

"Whoa," I jumped back on the couch, covering the forms with a book from school. "I've never seen lightning like that before."

Michael turned off the exhaust fan, the gas stove, and let out a mocking chuckle. He transferred the contents of his food from the wok he was cooking in to a ceramic serving bowl, and carefully placed it on a trivet on top of his pristine granite counter tops. I watched him as he set the table, perfectly. Methodically.

"I'm sure you have seen lightning like this," he tossed a dishtowel over the left shoulder of his burgundy button-down. "Just never at nearly forty stories up."

"It was still scary," I rolled my eyes and gathered my books into a pile on his coffee table. Smoothing down my jeans as I stood, I made my way over to the small bistro table near the kitchen. Thankfully, the table wasn't near any windows.

"You didn't answer my question," he stated, handing me a piping-hot bowl of food. "What were you working on while I was cooking?"

I was actually caught off guard by Michael's interest. Whenever he asked me personal questions, I just always assumed he was being polite. Trying to seem supportive, but not necessarily interested in what was going on in my life.

"I was just going over some notes from last week's lecture," I lied. I didn't want to tell him the truth. That Dr. Greenfield was making me enroll in psychoanalysis two days a week, out of fear he might grill me about therapy every week. Or worse, that he might think I am unstable.

"Getting a head start on midterms this semester?" he smiled, pouring a glass of pinot noir for us both.

I nodded my head, "Something like that." I desperately wanted to change the subject. "Thank you for cooking dinner, it smells amazing." I looked up at him through my lashes, giving him my best "aren't I adorable?" look. "You're such a good cook, baby."

"Thank you," he smiled, pulling out his chair. He let out a sigh as he lowered himself into the seat.

"Getting old?" I joked, picking up my wine glass. If he was getting old, he definitely didn't look it. He looked just as gorgeous as the day I met him. Even more so now that he was a few years older and his looks had matured a bit more.

"Yes," he responded with a straight face. "Twenty-four is killing me. Or maybe it's just being in this program."

I swallowed my wine. "Or maybe it's living in New York," I spat out.

I felt my eyes widen. It was completely out of my control. *Whoa! Where did that come from?*

He gave me an uneasy smile and took a bite of his risotto. He breathed in, as if he was about to say something, but then stopped himself.

Shaking my head, I forced a fast smile. "I don't know why I said that," I tried, laughing it off. I pursed my lips and shrugged my shoulders. "I love living in New York."

Michel paused for a minute and looked at me. "Do you?" he leaned forward, pushing the risotto around the bowl.

"Of course I do!" I answered with as much enthusiasm as I could muster up. "I probably just don't like living in Murray Hill."

He raised his eyebrows and chuckled slightly. "Well, I can't blame you for that." Resuming his normal demeanor he turned his attention back to his dinner.

I twirled my food around with my fork for a moment before taking a bite.

"Let me ask you a question," I uttered softly, suddenly nervous about his answer. "Do you ever think about moving out of New York?"

"No," he shook his head. He answered quickly and confidently. "All of the doctoral programs I applied to are here in New York. The furthest one is Hofstra University in Long Island. It's not in the city, but it's only about an hour on the train."

"Fair enough," I shrugged. "I mean, all of the programs I applied to are here in New York too." At this point, I was beginning to wonder if a doctoral program was the right choice for me. I figured it was just normal jitters of knowing I would be in school for at least five more years. I kept a smile plastered to my face as I continued to push my food around in my bowl. "I think what I mean is, after school is over. Do you ever see yourself moving to an area a little less urban?"

Michael just shook his head.

"Why not?" I asked, my worry growing with each reply.

"I can't imagine living anywhere else," he replied simply. "And honestly, I don't want to live anywhere else. This is my home."

"What about when you get married and have a family. Would you want to raise your children in the city?"

Michael put down his fork and looked up at me. He let out a sound that sounded like an exasperated sigh mixed with pity, and a slightly confused look crept onto his face. His lips pulled into a straight line and he looked as if he was choosing his words very carefully before speaking.

"I don't want kids," he formed each word slowly, with a sympathetic look on his face. A look that read, *I know you might want kids, but I will never want kids. So if we stay together that's something you'll have to give up.*

"Oh?" I said, but it came out more like a question. I was hoping he would explain his decision, but he just gave me another short smile and took a sip of his wine. I tried to hide the disappointment on my face. The truth was, I wasn't sure if I wanted to have kids either, but I was only twenty-four. I considered myself too young to know if I wanted them. In all seriousness, I hadn't had a free moment in the past two years to even think about having children. I did know one thing for certain, though. When the time was right, I wanted to get married. And I was sure that "want" would never go away.

"I guess we're really too young to be thinking about that stuff anyway," I conceded. Another crack of thunder followed by a laser light show of lightning filled the apartment. I jumped an inch in my chair and exhaled loudly. Michael seemed utterly unaffected by both the storm and our conversation.

"How do you like your dinner?" he looked up at me and smiled tightly. Obviously attempting to change the subject.

"It's honestly delicious, baby," I smiled back. I felt a weird vibe coming off him. Did he think I was unhappy with the food? I dabbed my mouth with the napkin and then folded my hands in my lap. "Thank you for cooking dinner."

"Someone has to," he mumbled. He reached for his drink and took a long sip.

I was taken aback by his comment. Stunned, I sat there as still as a statue. I couldn't tell if he was joking or not. His face remained neutral.

"Well, I just want you to know that I appreciate it." I tried to smooth it over. Michael just nodded and continued to eat in silence, his eyes fixed on his bowl.

I looked around Michael's pristine apartment. In the two years I had known him, the place hadn't changed a bit. Copper-toned pots and pans still hung elegantly from the ceiling in the kitchen as if they hadn't been touched since the first time I came over a few years ago. The small bistro table we were eating on hadn't moved an inch. Even the toothpaste in the bathroom was the same brand that it had always been. Michael was definitely a creature of habit, whereas I had already moved twice since graduating college. After spending high school in my hometown in Staten Island I went to college at Rutgers in New Jersey, and then moved here to Manhattan. I even moved to a new apartment after my first year here. Michael went to college here in Manhattan at Columbia, and then came downtown a bit to attend graduate school at NYU. I never asked him how long he had been living in this apartment, but it I realized it was probably somewhere around six years.

"Are you alright?" he asked, breaking me out of my daze.

I looked up at him, slowly taking it all in. He was so gorgeous. His brown eyes were soft with concern and his arm was stretched over the table so he could reach my hand. I felt my heart beat a little harder as we maintained eye contact.

I was so in love with him. The sheer force of it all consumed every ounce of me.

Sometimes it felt like a burden.

With a sheepish smile, I nodded, feeling myself bite on my bottom lip. Something I recently noticed I did when I got turned on. Which was essentially all of the time when I was with him.

Clearing my throat, I composed myself, running my fingers through my curls for a moment. I had a weird, anxious feeling in the pit of my stomach and I couldn't pinpoint where it was coming from. I struggled for conversation, resolving not to come off as boring.

"Oh! I have an idea," I shifted uncomfortably in my chair. "How about next Saturday you and I go to the Guggenheim Museum with Olivia and Alex. It could be a double date."

"Um, sure," he answered quickly, wiping his hands with his napkin. "I have some studying I have to do in the morning, so we would just have to go in the afternoon."

"I'm sure Olivia won't mind," I said quickly, trying to hide my huge grin. Our first double date. Things were definitely moving in the right direction. Maybe the anxiety was for nothing after all. Maybe if Michael saw how happy Olivia and Alex were, he'd want to finally be in a serious relationship with me. "I think it's going to be a good time."

Michel took the last bite of his food. I looked down and realized I had hardly eaten any of it. I wasn't that hungry, though. I took another sip of my wine and a final bite of my food. I stood up to clear the dishes, but Michael, as usual, stopped me.

"Amalia, you're in my home. You don't have to clean up."

"Maybe next weekend you can sleep at my apartment," I blurted out. "You know, after the museum."

Michel stopped in his tracks, his back still to me, and then slowly began to rinse out the bowls in the sink. "I'll let you know. I really have so much work to get done and it would take me over half an hour to get back here from your apartment Sunday morning. But we'll see how much I get done Saturday."

"Oh, alright," I mumbled in a near-whisper. "We'll figure it out."

Michael had never been to my new apartment before. The only time he had ever come to see me was last year to try and stop me from going to Brazil. At that point I was still living in the West Village.

I looked out the window. The rain looked like it was finally clearing up a bit, but it still looked gloomy and gray outside. Through the fog and the rain, the view of midtown Manhattan from Michael's window looked almost like a dystopian future. Colorless, cold, and uncertain. I shivered, looking for a blanket. I made my way over to the couch and pulled my knees up to my chest.

"Baby, I'm cold. Could I have a cup of tea?"

He finished loading the dishwasher and crossed over to me, putting his arm around my waist once he sat down.

"I have a better idea," he whispered, his voice low and velvety. His ardent tone gave me chills.

He lifted the tip of my chin up with his finger and ran his thumb softly over my lips right before leaning in to push his warm, pillowy lips into mine. My lips parted and he ran his tongue along the inside of my mouth, softly at first but then with more urgency. This was how most of our kisses were. Hard and fast. He pulled on my legs and before I knew it I was flat on my back. His hands were on my face, then on my breasts, on my legs, and then pulling at my jeans. I took the hint and removed my pants myself as he tugged on my sweater. As soon as my clothes were off, we went right back to kissing. We couldn't get enough of each other. It was like Michael was my drug, and each time we had sex I wanted more and more. As he started to kiss my neck, I immediately began unbuttoning his shirt. As soon as I removed it, I let out a soft moan in response to his perfectly toned arms and stomach. When did the guy ever have time to work out? A second later, he picked me up and carried me to his bedroom. I crawled on top of him and pulled off his pants.

For a split second, he held my gaze. He kissed me softly and then gently ran his fingertips down my face. I felt something I hadn't felt before with him; an overwhelming feeling of wanting to say *I love you*. I thought about saying it, but didn't. I didn't want to be the first one to say it. So, instead, I reached over him and grabbed a condom out of his nightstand. Even though I was on the pill, Michael wasn't my boyfriend, and I wasn't taking any chances that anything could go wrong. I raised my eyebrows and his eyes darkened as his pupils dilated from anticipation. I climbed back on top of him, reached over to the nightstand one last time, and turned off the light.

Ten – Olivia

"I haven't been to this museum in years," Alex said, tightly holding onto the railing on the train. The uptown line was crowded as all hell, and Alex held my waist tightly as a group of children with their parents kept bumping into me. I wasn't exactly a "kid" person, something I realized Alex and I would have to talk about before we got married. Oddly enough, I wasn't sure how many, or if he even wanted children of his own. There just never seemed like there was an opportunity to talk about it.

This weekend, like all weekends, had been absolutely hellacious for getting around the city. Alex and I had gone to Morandi for brunch down in the Village, and we were stopped every two minutes on our walk there by tourists asking for directions to Bleeker Street. There was no avoiding it, on the weekends any mode of transportation you chose meant having to deal with copious crowds of tourists.

"Should be fun," I said, shooting the mother of one of the rowdy little boys a little side-eye. She grimaced and then went back to talking to her friend. The train was so crowded I was beginning to feel dizzy.

"You sound very convinced," he lowered his eyes down to me and smirked.

"A double date with Amalia and Michael?" I scoffed, with a

sarcastic flair to my voice. I could tell the crowd was making me irritable. "I mean, come on, this isn't the Brady Bunch. Ten bucks says he doesn't even show up."

"Come on, Olivia. Now why would you say something like that?" Alex gave me a quick squeeze. "It sounds to me like you don't want Amalia and Michael dating."

The train stopped and after having ridden it all the way from Union Square, we finally were able to get off. I breathed a sigh of relief as the conductor called out our stop over the speaker. We left the crowded subway car for the crowded streets of the upper east side of Manhattan. As soon as we reached the top of the subway terminal and got onto the street, I could smell the pretzels and warm nuts being sold on every other street corner. The cold wind swirled around us and I quickly retrieved my gloves from my coat pocket.

"Because I just don't see them as a couple," I shrugged, leading us toward the museum. "Which, to be frank, they aren't. How long have they been doing this back-and-forth dance now? As far as I know, he hasn't told her he wants to be exclusive, and I wouldn't be surprised if that day never comes." I knew I was bordering on rambling, but I felt very over-protective of Amalia. After seeing her get her heart broken so badly by Nicholas, I couldn't bear the idea of my best friend going through a similar situation. "I know Michael is your friend, so please don't repeat this, but I honestly feel like she should have chosen Hayden over Michael. They seemed much happier together. *She* seemed much happier"

Alex nodded, seemingly unaffected by my rant. He reached for my hand and asked, "Do you ever think you should have chosen someone else over me?"

The question caught me so off guard that I couldn't help but laugh. "If only you could see inside my head, you'd never have to ask me that question again."

But would you choose someone else over me?

I stopped walking for a minute and stood on my toes to offer

61

him a kiss. "There's no one I would choose over you, darling." Alex was at least five inches taller than me, towering over me whenever I wasn't wearing heels. Which was most times.

He kissed me back, and then kissed my hand. Even with my gloves on, I still loved when he kissed my hand. Although it was about forty-five degrees on this chilly October day, the wind in the city made it feel more like thirty-five. But I felt safe and warm with my loving fiancé by my side. We walked a few more chilly blocks until we reached the entrance to the Guggenheim Museum. Amalia was already waiting outside, craning her neck to look around. I checked my watch; Alex and I were right on time.

"Hey!" I called out to her. She smiled broadly and waved at us. We crossed the street, nearly getting hit by a group of teenage boys on skateboards.

"How's it going, Hastings?" Alex asked, actually leaning over to give her a small hug.

Amalia made a weird face, but accepted Alex's hug, her tiny frame disappearing next to him.

"Um, dude. Did you really just hug me?" she asked with a suspicious tone.

"It surprised me too," he shrugged.

"So, is Michael here yet?" I asked, looking around the crowd of tourists and families.

Amalia rubbed her gloveless hands together in an effort to generate some heat. I noticed her nails were freshly painted. Her hair was straightened, which was rare for her. Usually she kept her blonde locks in their natural curly state. Her make-up was a little heavier than usual, and a bit inappropriate for three o'clock in the afternoon. Anyone who knew her could tell she was trying to look good. Trying hard. I felt the excitement come off her in waves as she held a wide smile, which was shining with bright red lip-gloss.

"He should be here any minute," she practically sang. "I'm so glad you could come, I am sure you're so busy planning the wedding!"

I opened my mouth to answer, but luckily Alex cut me off.

"It's coming along," Alex answered for us. "It's good to get out of the apartment." I was grateful. I knew Amalia wouldn't ask him a ton of questions, and I wasn't one of those brides who constantly wanted to talk about their wedding plans. Planning was stressful enough without having to talk about them all of the time.

A few more minutes of small talk went by, the whole time Amalia kept the smile frozen to her face. I looked around the street one more time, and had the sinking feeling that the sarcastic bet I made with Alex on the subway was taking fruition. Michael wasn't just running late. He wasn't coming. A beat later, Amalia's cell began to ring. She retrieved it from her back pocket and told us it was a text message from Michael. As soon as she began reading it, her entire face dropped. She pursed her lips and then slid the cell back into her pocket. Her eyes looked glassy and I silently willed her not to start crying. She had on way too much make-up to start any amount of water works.

Alex and I exchanged a glance, and for a moment he looked as if he genuinely felt sorry for her.

"Are you okay?" I muttered, already knowing the answer to the question.

"He, um-" she began to stammer. Taking a deep breath, she continued. "He can't make it. Something about having too much work to get done and apologizes to the two of you for his absence."

"The amount of work we get can definitely cut into our social lives," Alex offered an explanation. I shot him a look. Even though he was probably just trying to be helpful, I could tell that was the last thing Amalia wanted to hear right now.

I expected her to come back at him with a snappy comment, but she didn't. She just looked at the floor, concentrating on a piece of gum that had most likely been stuck there since Giuliani was mayor.

"I'm sorry he couldn't make it," I said, with a little too much pity in my voice. "But I promise we can still have fun, just the three of us." I looked at Alex to make sure he was okay with that plan. He nodded in agreement.

"No, I don't think I'm going to go in," she shook her head. She reached into her purse and pulled out a pair of fuzzy ear muffs. She ran her fingers over the faux fur as she continued to fight back tears. Her eyes were red from both the cold and the emotion.

I felt horrible for her.

She shuffled her feet a bit and crossed her arms in front of her chest. "The two of you should go and have a good day, but I am just going to head home."

"Are you sure?" Alex asked. My eyes widened at the sound of his voice. He must really have felt bad for Amalia if he was being this nice to her. She probably realized that, because as soon as he finished talking, she let out a drawn-out sigh.

"I'm sure," she put on her ear muffs. "I'll see you guys on Monday."

Without another word, she scuttled over to the street corner and managed to get a cab right away.

I turned to Alex. "I'm such a bitch," I rubbed my forehead.

"What?"

"What I said on the subway. How he probably wouldn't even show up. I never should have said that."

"It's not as if you saying that changed the course of the universe and made him decide not to come, Olivia."

"I don't know what to do with her," I said, surprised at my own words. "Michael is a good guy, but he's not good to Amalia." I stopped walking and faced Alex. "Do you think I should sit her down and try to explain this to her?"

He pressed his lips into a straight line. "If she's in love with him, there is nothing you or anyone else can say that will make her leave him. It's something she has to feel for herself."

I nodded, knowing deep down that he was right. "So what should we do now? Do you want to go inside?"

"Not really," he answered.

"Me neither."

We paused for a moment, both knowing we had to think of something else to do. We had come in all of the way from Roosevelt Island to hang out with them.

Alex reached for my hand. "Let's just grab a cup of coffee somewhere and talk."

"That sounds nice," I agreed. "Under one condition."

"What's that?" we started walking away from the museum.

"That we don't talk about anything stressful for one whole hour."

I took a deep breath, feeling the cold air constrict my throat. "Sold."

Eleven – Amalia

I knew there was a chance I'd regret this, but I couldn't help it. Michael had left me hanging, essentially stood me up, and embarrassed me in front of our closest friends.

I was mortified.

I can't remember how long it had been since Hayden had sent me the text message in which he asked if we could be friends. At the time, it seemed like a terrible idea. I always thought being friends with an "ex" was a recipe for disaster. I looked at it as a selfish excuse for keeping someone in your life without offering them anything other than a watered-down version of what you used to mean to each other. And if you're not careful, you'll end up having sex with them, ruining said friendship. How could you get over them or keep your dignity in tact while experiencing them moving on to another?

But I didn't care about any of that right now. Cassandra was gone, my relationship with my parents was basically non-existent, I hadn't spoken to my brother in months, and who knows what was going on between Michael and me. Not to mention having to watch Olivia and Alex being the perfect couple all of the time was making me feel more than a little uncomfortable in my own skin.

I was walking fast, weaving in and out of crowds of tourists as I made a beeline for the subway. As the harsh wind hit my face over and over again, feeling like a slap of reality with each gust. This is who Michael had always been, and possibly who he always would be. I pulled myself over and dug around in my purse for my cell phone and a hair tie. I found my phone and immediately opened my messages. Of course, there was nothing more from Michael. I hadn't even written him back after he told me he couldn't make it. I honestly had nothing to say. We weren't officially a couple, and this was one of those grey areas where I wasn't sure how much disappointment or anger I was allowed to show him. Instead of composing a passive-aggressive text to him, or possibly an all-out aggressive one, I decided to text someone else altogether.

I scrolled through my message threads until I found Hayden's name and clicked on it. It was a Sunday afternoon and I expected him to be out with a friend, or possibly on a date, but I took my chances and shot him a text.

"Hey! Hope you're doing well. Sorry it took me so long to write back but if you're still up for it, I'd like to try this whole "friendship" thing. It's short notice, but I'm free this afternoon if you're around."

As I waited for Hayden's response, I opened the Facebook application on my phone and went directly to Michael's profile. I absentmindedly scrolled through his timeline, which was pretty scarce. He hardly ever updated anything; just a few statuses about his favorite football team, the New York Giants.

I swiftly moved my fingers from his timeline up to his photos. I had never really gone through his profile page with a fine tooth comb, but for some reason today I felt the need to. There are moments in relationships where you feel like you know absolutely nothing about the person you've shared so much with. This was one of those times.

There were two albums: one labeled "family" and one labeled "miscellaneous". I started with the album called "family" and scrolled my way through a dozen photos of him, his parents, and his sister. This was the first time I had ever seen photos of them, and it had just occurred to me that I didn't even know his parents' names. I clicked on one of the photos to find out, but neither his mother nor father was tagged in them, so I had no way of knowing. I let out a sigh and moved on to the other album. This one was much smaller, only about five photos. One of him and Alex standing outside of NYU's Bobst Library, the picture being most likely taken by Olivia. The rest of the photos were of him and his ex-girlfriend, Marge. The girl he had been cheating on with me. I winced as I remembered her slapping me across the face last year. A couple of the photos were taken in front of the tree in Rockefeller Center from a couple of years ago, but the rest were taken in Phoenix, Arizona. Adding insult to injury, my eyes scanned the photos of them comfortably lounging on outdoor furniture, donning sunglasses and holding frosty mugs in the hot Phoenix sun. I felt tears well up behind my eyes as I thought about Michael flying across the country to visit Marge, but unable to make it uptown to spend a few hours with me at a museum.

Just as one warm tear hit my ice-cold cheek, my phone vibrated with a reply from Hayden.

"Hi, Amalia! It's great to hear from you. I'm actually free this evening if you want to grab a bite to eat…"

I gasped. I expected a terse, apprehensive answer. What I got was a warm welcome. Something I wasn't used to in my everyday life.

I wasn't sure what to do. Going out to eat seemed much more formal than grabbing a cup of coffee. I definitely didn't want to mislead Hayden into thinking my intentions for seeing him were romantic. I deliberated for a few more minutes until I finally came up with a good idea. I tried to type quickly, but my fingers were getting more frozen by the second. After three autocorrects, I hit send.

"Sure – how about the downtown Rosa Mexicana?"

I felt a mixture of guilt and excitement over seeing Hayden. Truth be told, I had no reason to feel guilty about it. We were going to try to be friends, that's all. Come to think of it, I don't think Michael would mind even if he and I *were* exclusive. I got the feeling that when it comes to Michael, it takes a lot for him to let his guard down and show any true emotions. I took a deep breath as I realized I wasn't exactly being honest with Michael about my own feelings. I was hurt when he didn't show up at the museum. And not because he was too busy, those things happen and our program is extremely difficult. I was hurt and angry because of the way he handled it. A simple text message? At the very least, he could have called me and pretend to sound disappointed that we couldn't spend the day together.

When it came to my feelings for Michael, I was so happy to even be seeing him on a regular basis that I was afraid a fight would destroy any chance of a future together, so I held my tongue. On the same token, we had been dating for a few months now and there still had been no talk of putting a label on what we were doing.

Then for a brief moment, I let my mind drift over to Dr. Greenfield and what he had said about going to therapy.

I stared at the subway entrance, desperately willing Hayden to write me back quickly so I could get on the train and head back to my apartment. I was growing colder by the second. Whoever said autumn in New York was beautiful?

A beat later, my phone vibrated with a message from Hayden. He had written that Rosa Mexicana sounded great and that he'd meet me there at seven. I shot off a quick, *"See you there!"* and hauled ass down into the subway entrance, determined to take a warm nap before meeting him for dinner.

I arrived at Rosa Mexicana, the one in Union Square, at seven o'clock on the dot and was immediately greeted with the smell of warm tortilla chips, sizzling fajitas, and grilled vegetables. My mouth instantly began to water.

I looked around the brightly colored restaurant hoping to spot Hayden. I was just about to take a seat on the wooden bench by the host stand when I found him sitting at the bar. He looked exactly the same as I remembered him. Light-brown hair, casually dressed in a button-down with the sleeves rolled up, somehow always looking casual but still having great style. To top it all off was, of course, the signature glass of bourbon in his hand. He sipped it slowly as he patiently waited for me to walk over to him. He wasn't checking his phone or nervously looking around the room. He seemed calm. Relaxed. I smiled, and in nothing flat found my own shoulders relax as well.

"How many?" a tall lanky host dressed in all black asked.

"Two," I replied. "But is it alright if we eat at the bar?"

"Of course," he smiled politely.

I slowly made my way over to Hayden, growing more anxious with every step. I had no idea what this conversation was going to be like, or how to even begin. Should I give him a hug? A handshake? Or should I just sit right down and make some snappy comment on something. As I approached the bar area, I noticed only a few other people were sitting down. Most of the restaurant's patrons had opted for a booth or table, giving us two some privacy. A beat later I was standing right behind him and realized that I had no idea what I was doing.

"Amalia," he said my name softly and unhesitatingly stood up to hug me. "It's so great to see you." He lifted me slightly off the ground as he hugged me. I could feel the bottoms of my shoes gently graze the floor. Slowly, he released me from the hug a a nd took a step back. His eyes scanned every inch of me, but not in a creepy way. It actually seemed as if he had seem a ghost.

"Hi, Hayden," I uttered through a shaky voice. I glanced down and realized my voice wasn't the only thing that was shaking. My hands looked at if someone had just asked me to dismantle an atomic bomb. I quickly put my arms behind my back and took a step backwards.

The bartender crossed over to us and raised his eyebrows, indicating that I should order.

"Can I have a glass of sangria, please?" There was no way I could get through this encounter without some alcohol.

The bartender gave me a quick nod and walked towards the other side of the bar. I pulled out the empty high-top chair next to Hayden and placed my jacket and purse on the back. Hayden reached for my arm, helping me hop onto the stool, which was surprisingly high. Buying myself time to calm my nerves, I smoothed over my clothes and ran my fingers through my hair. As soon as I did so, I remembered that my usual curls were straightened in an attempt to look good for Michael. My feelings switched from sadness to anger as I re-lived the embarrassment of him not coming to the museum. The bartender came back with my drink and placed it down in front of me and I muttered a low thank you.

"How have you been?" I finally uttered. Hayden seemed happy to see me, but I was still expecting some pent-up resentment for me ditching him for Michael back in February.

"Honestly?" he raised an eyebrow. He took his drink in his hand and swirled the amber-colored liquid. "I'm alright, I guess." He offered me a smile, but I could see in his eyes that he wasn't in a good place.

"Just alright?" my heart started to race. I knew this was the moment that Hayden was going to let me have it.

He shrugged one shoulder and then nodded. "Work's been going well," he paused to take a sip of his drink. His eyes stayed fixed on the wooden bar. "So well, in fact, that they've offered me a promotion."

"That's great!" I patted him on the back and he gave me a weak smile. "Why don't you seem more excited about it?"

He shook his head. "I know I should be. I've enjoyed my time at Ernst and Young so far, and now I'll be in an even better position there. It comes with a raise and even a company car."

"A car?" I laughed. "What would you do with a car in New York City?"

Hayden looked straight into my eyes and I felt my heart sink. "The job isn't in New York City. If I take the offer, I would be relocating."

It was always shocking to me when people leave New York. It's something everyone at one point or another says they're going to do, but hardly anyone really does. I think they subconsciously know that if they had to leave the city, they would have no other choice than to actually cut the crap and grow up.

I swirled the tiny straw in my Sangria. "Where is the job located? New Jersey?"

He let out a soft chuckle. "No, it's a little farther than that. Ironically the company wants to move me into their Gainesville office." He kept his eyes on his drink, but didn't take a sip. "It's funny, really, I spent so many years trying to make it in New York and it looks like now I may be moving back home."

"To Florida?" the word caught in my throat and I felt my face drop. Hayden was thinking about moving a thousand miles away.

"The opportunity sort of presented itself at a perfect time," he added, and then finally took a small sip of his bourbon. "I've been thinking about leave New York for the past couple of months now."

"Why move?" was all I could muster up.

He cleared his throat and looked back to my eyes. I didn't know if it was the stress of the city or something else going on in his life, but for the first time I really felt that Hayden was older than me. As he maintained eye contact, he donned a forced smile. I felt sorry for him. He wasn't the same Hayden I knew anymore. He seemed broken.

"Because there's no reason for me to stay," he replied simply. "There's nothing left for me here."

I looked down at the floor as I tried to think of something persuasive to say, but I came up with nothing. Hayden had always been flexible when it came to living in this city. Unlike Olivia and Alex, who I was positive would only move out of New York after their second child was born, Hayden was more untethered than that. Just as I was a native New Yorker he was a native of Florida, and to him that would always be his true home.

"What about your friends here?" I asked, pulling at straws. "Won't you miss them?"

Hayden shook his head. "They're my coworkers. Sure, I grab a beer with some of them every now and then. But they're acquaintances at best." He wasn't looking at me again, and I wondered as he was telling me if this was the first time he ever really thought about his friendships. "It's not very easy to make new friends in your late twenties." He lifted his eyes again. Each glance in my direction made me feel nervous.

"I guess I can understand that," I offered. "It's different for me because of NYU. But I can relate to some of how you're feeling." I took a pause and suddenly felt the urge to take a long sip of my sangria. "For example, Cassandra doesn't even speak to me anymore."

I would usually feel my eyes threaten to tear whenever I thought about my best friend and me no longer speaking. This time was different; I didn't feel like crying. Oddly, I didn't feel much of anything at all.

Hayden opened his mouth to say something, but the bartender cut in.

"Are you guys ready to order?" he leant over the bar, his eyes rolling over to our menus.

"Just a few more minutes," I said.

The bartender nodded and scurried back to the other side of the bar, which was suddenly packed with customers.

"What happened between you and Cassandra?" Hayden asked in a sympathetic voice.

It had occurred to me that the only other person I had talked to about Cassie was Olivia. Even Michael wasn't privy to my feeling about Cassandra and me falling out. I started at the beginning, how last year when she picked me up from the airport, she seemed more interested in partying on Fire Island than she was in seeing

73

her best friend who had been gone for a few months. I went on to describe everything that she had done. Her aloof behavior, the party Olivia and I had attended which I called Hayden to come and rescue me from. I went through all of it, right up to the time I had seen her at the Union Square farmers' market and she turned the other way.

"This has been going on for *that* long?" a look of surprise taking over his face. "How come you never told me about all of this while we were dating?"

That was a good question. Why hadn't I told Hayden about Cassandra's neglect of our friendship? Even when I would talk to Olivia about it, it would be a brief complaint and then a quick change of subject.

"I think I'm beginning to realize that I'm not very good at handling my emotions, Hayden." I felt my shoulders sink in this moment of self-reflection. "But you probably already know that, seeing as I ran away from you in February." I stared at my cuticles, ashamed at my past behavior.

Hayden looked at the floor and then took a deep breath, repositioning himself on the chair.

"I'm sorry about that," I said as earnestly as possible. "That was cowardly of me."

He pursed his lips and gave a small nod. I couldn't tell if he was agreeing with me or simply uncomfortable with this conversation.

"Are you with Michael now?" he asked in a shaky voice.

"We're dating, yes. But we aren't in a relationship yet."

"How come?"

I paused for a moment, running my fingers over the shiny menu. "He wants to take things slow."

Hayden just nodded. I could tell he didn't want any more information on the topic, so I didn't offer any. He picked up his menu from the bar and flipped it open. "So, what's good here?" he smiled.

I hesitated for a moment and then said, "Everything." Relieved to be essentially off the hook, I followed suit and picked up my menu. The bartender began to walk by again but I held up one finger, indicating we would be ready in just a minute.

"Do you know what you want?" I asked, closing my plastic menu.

For a moment our eyes locked and I felt a familiar feeling wash over me. It was the feeling I had always had with Hayden. Complete comfort.

"Yep." He smiled again, this time it felt genuine. He folded his paper napkin and placed it on his lap. "Do you, Amalia?"

"Yeah," I shrugged.

"Well, then," he chuckled before taking a sip of bourbon. "That's a first."

Twelve – Olivia

Halloween was this up-coming weekend, which meant one thing here in New York City.

Disaster.

The city took on a life of its own, pulsating with the energy of inebriated twenty-somethings.

Being obsessed with holidays and everything that went along with them, Alex had, of course, procured our costumes nearly a month ago. He decided we would be characters from *Game of Thrones*, his favorite show, and I agreed. For my costume I would be donning a platinum-blonde wig and a light-blue dress with a metallic belt around the waist, dressed up of course as Khaleesi, Mother of Dragons. I wasn't sure what he was going to be wearing, but I believed it to be a toned-down version of a knight costume. Chain metal was pretty heavy. To make matters worse we would be attending the opening night at some club I had never heard of, in a part of town I dreaded. Morningside Heights. This is a neighborhood in Manhattan that spans from West 110th to 125th. If you looked on a map, you could see it stretching from the east end of Morningside Park to the Hudson River.

During the daytime, it's not so bad. There have been many bars, restaurants and tourist attractions added to make the neighbor-hood safer. Not to mention the prestigious Columbia University on West 116th street. However, there is still a pretty high crime rate around the area. Fortunately, the party was located not too far from Columbia's campus, so I figured we would be safe.

Alex was grabbing lunch with Michael so I had the whole place to myself. I had to admit I was driving myself crazy wondering if Michael was *really* his lunch date. After seeing that unknown red-head girl in the park, I had been thinking of ways to ask Alex about it. The timing just never seemed right.

I slowly walked around my and Alex's apartment, idly running my fingers over everything in my path. The kitchen counters, the high back stools, the sofa in the sitting area. I made my way into the bedroom. Even though this was my new home, the entire apartment still felt like Alex's. We were waiting for the lease to be up before putting the apartment in both of our names. Hopefully Alex wouldn't change his mind about our upcoming nuptials and kick me out, leaving me essentially homeless. Kind of like how Amalia was last year before moving to Murray Hill.

Right down to the closets, which held meticulously pressed button-down shirts, and a suit in every color imaginable, the bedroom felt like him. I looked down at my own outfit, skinny jeans and an over-sized fair-isle sweater from the Gap. Not exactly couture. I sighed and crossed over to the bed. The sheets were incredibly soft, at least 800 thread count. I ran my fingers over the burgundy-colored duvet and pillowcases, both equally as soft as the sheets.

Sitting on the edge of the bed, I glanced out of the window, which offered me a stunning panoramic view of the Manhattan skyline. I smiled in awe of the city. I never got tired of that view.

Looking down at my ring, I watched as light danced off the diamond, making it sparkle in a way I had never noticed before. It was truly beautiful, and in moments like this I couldn't believe it was mine. I thought about how chaotic everything had been in Rhode Island. My parents' constant arguing would send me running. I would often drive to an empty spot by one of the marinas and sit on the dock, dreaming of the day I would be able to run away from that life. To escape.

And praying that my life never included the sadness that had beset them.

Looking out at the city now, I realized I had gotten exactly that. I had been given a whole new life, and next year I would be married. Married, living on Roosevelt Island, and hopefully enrolled in a doctoral program. If I was really lucky, Alex and I would be accepted on the same program and we would be able to attend school together again. But I knew that was improbable. All of the programs were small, the largest of them accepted twenty students. I knew I had a better shot at NYU than anywhere else, if only because I would have already obtained my Master's there. Not to mention the weekly boredom that came from working with Dr. Greenfield. The work-study program had better provide me with a glowing letter of recommendation.

I looked at my ring one more time, holding my hand up to the sunlight. It was a little hard to believe that in May I'd be wearing a graduation cap and gown, and in July I'd be in a wedding dress. A smile tugged at my lips as I slowly laid my head on the softest pillow I had ever felt.

Thirteen – Amalia

The day before Halloween I sat on a comfortable, oversized chair, twirling my frizzy curls as a doctoral student sat in a less-than-comfortable-looking chair directly across from me. As I played with the strands of my blonde hair, the first thought that came to mind was how overdue I was for some highlights. Already bored, one minute into therapy (only thirty-nine more minutes to go), I turned my eyes onto the girl-playing-therapist. She had naturally red hair, not the kind that came in a bottle you'd see on sale at Target for ten bucks. Her skin was fair, even more pale then my own. She was dressed in a form-fitting pencil skirt, a flowing ivory-colored blouse, and kitten heels. As I studied the person who would be in turn studying me for the remainder of my tenure at NYU, I concluded that she was around twenty-nine years old. Initially, her appearance reminded me of the old Dolly Parton song, "Jolene."

Feeling both annoyed and impatient, I leaned back in my chair a bit and folded my arms. I was still reeling from the fact that Dr. Greenfield was making me do this. I asked Olivia and August about it, and neither of them was being forced to talk to a stranger. My eyes fixed on the clipboard she clutched in her hands, undoubtedly to be used to write down my every thought. At the ripe old age of twenty-nine, how much more about life could she possible know than me? Her chocolate- brown eyes were somehow warm and challenging at the same time. I couldn't tell how tall she was from sitting down, but I could tell that she was quite thin. About five to ten pounds thinner than me, at least. Finally, after a good five more minutes of us looking at one another, she wrote something down on her clipboard and smiled.

"So, Amelia," she began, uncrossing and then recrossing her thin legs.

"Amalia," I corrected her, my arms still folded in front of my chest.

"That's right," she nodded, her expression remaining the same. "'Amalia Danette Hastings,'" she overly enunciated my name before offering me another smile. "I apologize."

She sure didn't look sorry. In fact, she looked smug. Even a tad elitist.

"It's cool," I shrugged, resolving not to let her get to me. "You can just call me Amalia, though. It sounds like I have a fancy title when you say my entire name out loud like that." I lowered my eyes to the ground, but my attention was grabbed by her footwear. Before now I hadn't noticed the red soles brightly displayed on the bottom of her kitten heels. Louboutins, just like Cassandra always wore. I felt a wave of bitter resentment flow through me, starting at my own shoes that I had gotten on sale at Macy's. The counselor's shoes easily cost nine times what I paid for mine. Frustrated already, hot tears threatened to come out through my eyes, which were undoubtedly markedly glassy and red.

I did *not* want to be here.

It was bad enough I was forced into this arrangement by Dr. Greenfield, but did he really need to sit me across from some type-A super-model? Were there no nice guys in the program I could have been paired with? This girl obviously came from, or made, a great deal of money. How could she possibly relate to my life in any real way?

"Amalia," she started again, leaning in a little closer to me this time. "What brings you here today?"

"Well-" I started. "I'm sorry but I didn't catch your name. That's probably an important thing to tell your clients. No?" I smirked and finally unfolded my arms, letting them relax onto my lap.

For a slight moment, her tight smile twitched. Her eyes darted to the floor and then back up to me so fast you'd have missed it if you'd blinked. Checkmate. I wasn't the only one to sit there being uncomfortable for the next few months.

"My name is Autumn Mercer," she replied, and then took the opportunity to jot something down on her clipboard.

"Your first name is Autumn?" I shifted in my chair. The sheer size of the thing felt as if it was swallowing me whole. I kicked my legs up and decided to sit cross-legged. I didn't care that I had put my shoes on it – maybe a few stains would help convince the faculty to chuck it for a new one.

"It's my middle name," Autumn shrugged. My first name is Lauren, but a teacher read my middle name out loud during attendance one day in high school and it just kind of stuck." As if realizing she had offered up too much information, she straightened her posture and lifted her chin a bit. "Now you officially know more about me than I do about you, Amalia."

I glared back at her. "What do you want to know, Autumn?"

"Let's start with you telling me a little bit about yourself." She placed the clipboard and held her hands open, a gesture for me to feel free to talk. "Where did you grow up? What kind of person are you?"

"Don't you already have that information from the form I filled out?"

"I'd prefer to hear you tell me about it," she pressed on.

Exasperated by this conversation, I rubbed my tired eyes. I still couldn't believe I was going to be going to therapy once a week until April. That seemed like decades from now.

"Well I guess I am a pretty normal person," I offered.

"What do you think makes someone normal?" she quickly replied.

81

Taken aback by the question, I involuntarily scrunched my face. I thought about it for a second. What was a good answer I could give this girl so she'd get off my case and move on to something else?

"I believe what makes someone normal is the absence of any diagnostic criteria that would categorize them as having a developmental or mental disorder. Someone who is not in the clinical population," I spat out, sounding like an intro-to-psychology textbook.

Autumn didn't answer me. Instead, she sat still for a moment before scribbling something onto her paper. When she was finished she folded her hands and placed them on her lap. She was so reserved, I immediately found it bothersome.

"Is something wrong?" I uttered.

"I'm just thinking about your answer," she touched her hand to her chin and grimaced. "There is certain so-called *diagnostic criteria* that anyone can relate to.

"Such as?" I challenged.

"Anxiety, for one," she uncrossed her legs and leaned forward. "Tell me, Amalia, do you ever experience any anxiety?"

"Of course," I shrugged. There was a slight edge to my voice, but I didn't care.

"But wouldn't that be a deciding factor in diagnosing a disorder?" she inquired. She ran her fingers through her red hair and pulled it all over to one side of her shoulder. She seemed like an overly confident person and I smiled to myself as I realized I was probably analyzing her more than she was me.

"I'm not in school to become a psychologist," I muttered, in a recalcitrant tone.

"Humor me," she said in a low voice.

I shook my head but still played along. "Everyone experiences anxiety," I said plainly. A satisfied smile spread across her pore-less face. "However, if I *were* studying to become a psychologist, I would know that there is a difference between a casual case of the jitters and the pervasive oppression of living with an anxiety disorder."

Autumn kept her smug smile pinned to her face. "You're very clever, aren't you?"

"Am I?" I asked. "Or do I just not like someone suggesting I may not be normal."

"That's not what I did."

I rolled my eyes and looked past Autumn to the digital clock she had sitting on her desk. Our time was almost up. I took a deep breath and slowly let it out.

"To answer your other question," I looked her straight in the eyes, I wanted to show her she wasn't as intimidating as she liked to think she was. "I grew up in Staten Island. I'm a native New Yorker, and my parents are native New Yorkers too. They're from Queens."

"I didn't ask about your parents," she pursed her lips.

"No," I answered. "Not yet."

Autumn let out a defeatist sigh and leaned back into her chair. "You're not going to get anything out of being here if you don't at least try to participate."

"The only reason I am here is because Dr. Greenfield told me my placement in the work-study program was contingent upon me coming to analysis," I said emphatically. "I don't want to be here. This isn't a personal attack on you." I pointed at her for emphasis. "I need to remain in the program or I won't have any money to pay for, well, anything."

She tucked her hair behind her ears and raised an eyebrow, obviously not used to having such a difficult client. "Regardless of the reasons that brought you here, it will go by a lot faster if you stop fighting me. I'm not your enemy."

"Is this the part where you ask me if I think people are plotting against me?" I scrunched my eyebrows.

Autumn let out a small laugh and sighed. "No, I wasn't going to ask that. But you did bring up something I'd like to talk about."

"What's that?"

"You mentioned you weren't in school for psychology," she said.

"That's true," I said. "I'm not."

"There are a few paths to follow with the degree you're going for. In fact, it's pretty broad."

I nodded in agreement, unsure of where this conversation was heading.

"So, that in mind," she stood up and walked over to her desk, "And the fact that you're graduating in May, shouldn't you know by now what you want to do in terms of a career?"

I felt a spike in my blood pressure so palpable, for a moment I thought I was surely going into coronary arrest. This uptight bitch presumed to know so much about me. In any other situation, I would curse her out, but not this time. I was powerless, controlled by the threat of getting kicked out of my program. Controlled by Dr. Greenfield and his red-headed puppet.

Only I was the one attached to the strings.

"Thank you for bringing that to my attention. I'll be sure to think about what we discussed here before our next session." I spoke softly and measured, positive little Miss Mercer was trying to get a reaction out of me.

Unflappable, Autumn simply nodded before saying, "Our time is up."

I stood up, gathering my jacket and handbag in the process. I turned on my heel and reached for the doorknob, but before I could exit, she had to make one last remark.

"Ms. Hastings," she called.

"Yes, Ms. Mercer?" I said in a saccharine-sweet voice, not bothering to turn around.

"Have a safe and happy Halloween." I could hear the smirk on her face.

Without another word I walked out of her office, deliberately leaving the door open so she'd have to get up to close it.

Fourteen – Olivia

"Ouch!" I tripped over my heels for the third time. It was hard enough to walk in these shoes, not to mention it was pitch black out and freezing. There really was no such thing as autumn in New York.

"Why on earth did you pick those shoes?" Amalia asked, as she and I quickly headed further downtown than either of us wanted to go. "You usually wear flats or ankle boots. I didn't even know you owned strappy sandals. And gold ones on top of that!"

She made a good point. Why was I wearing these shoes? Oh, right. The same reason I was currently donning a platinum-blonde wig and carrying around a stuffed dragon in my purse.

Halloween really brought out the crazy in all of us.

We dragged ourselves all the way uptown, passing a few sketchy areas on the way to our destination. Distracted by my aching feet, I was completely thrown off balance when Amalia yanked on my arm, pulling me out of the way of a subway grate in the middle of the sidewalk. One wrong step in these heels and I'd twist my ankle before this party even started. I looked at her again and studied her choice of costume. Alex and I were going as characters from *Game of Thrones*, but Amalia didn't say anything about Michael and her coordinating outfits.

Michael and Alex were meeting us at the club, the name of

which I still couldn't remember, because they said they had to do something beforehand. I assumed it was bachelor-party planning. Amalia and I walked downtown together to keep each other company, and possibly, safe.

"Who are you supposed to be, again?" I asked, dodging her shiny black wings as she strutted down the avenue. A group of teenagers trotted by us, covered in shaving cream and silly string. One of them was smoking. I felt every muscle in my body ache as my brain screamed at me to ask him to bum one. I shook my head and whispered "no" to myself.

"I'm a dark fairy," she said, as if it were obvious. Bright-pink fake eyelashes adhered to her eyelids like tiny flower petals. As she spoke, the moonlight hit her mouth just right and I could see how shiny her blood-red lip-gloss was. It reminded me of how she was dressed at the museum. She was trying too hard.

Her usual curls were flat-ironed into a pin-straight sheet of blonde. She was wearing a black and purple dress that frayed out at the hem, sort of like a gothic version of Tinkerbelle's. To pull it together she wore a heavy dose of kohl eyeliner, black tights, and shiny black boots that laced up to her knee. Not to mention the broad wings, which appeared to be sown into the back of her dress.

"Amalia, are you wearing those wings all night?" I fiddled with my wig, already feeling itchy.

"Of course," she bounced along the sidewalk, oblivious to groups of people, who were ducking out of her way. I wondered how she would fit through the doorway.

"You're going to take an eye out," I chuckled.

"Yes, your grace," she muttered.

"What is Michael wearing tonight?" I asked softly, hoping not to cause an emotional eruption.

"I don't know," she said in a quiet, monotone voice. She didn't offer up any other information. I pressed my lips into a flat line, searching for the right words to say.

"Are the two of you in a fight?"

"No," she uttered

She wasn't looking at me, and upon closer examination she didn't look sad. She was eerily calm, a blank stare in her blue eyes. I let out a sigh and decided not to ask her any more questions about Michael tonight.

We turned the corner on 117th street and finally saw our destination. Although I didn't know the name of the club, it was the only building on the block with a line halfway around the corner. Alex had picked this venue and apparently shelled out some cash and got us on the guest list so the four of us wouldn't have to wait in line. As we made our way up to the bouncer, Amalia stopped walking and looked right at me. She had a sullen look on her face but her posture was still straight and strong.

"I hung out with Hayden the other day," she said in a flat, emotionless voice. "Michael still hasn't asked me to be exclusive, and I hung out with my ex-boyfriend the other day."

I didn't know what to say. I just stared at her.

"Oh! And the best part is, Hayden tells me he is moving back to Florida because he got this amazing job offer with Ernst and Young," she spat out. Her eyes were growing redder, but it didn't look like she was going to cry, she looked angry.

And possibly a little insane.

She took a few more steps toward the entrance. "Everyone's life is moving forward. Everyone's except mine."

Before I could answer her, she muttered our names to the bouncer and he lifted up the rope and waved us in. I numbly followed her lead, shocked at the news she had just told me. What was she doing hanging out with Hayden after all she had gone through to be with Michael?

A chorus of groans from the long line of people waiting to get into the club erupted as we stepped inside. The inside of the club was ominously dark and Halloween-themed. A cloud of white smoke surrounded our feet as Michael Jackson's "Thriller" blasted through the speakers. I grabbed Amalia's hand so we wouldn't get separated. It was ten o'clock and the place was already packed. I felt a slight wave of anxiety. The music was incredibly loud, the strobe lights kept flickering from orange to white, and I couldn't spot Alex anywhere. I turned to Amalia and shrugged my shoulders, unsure of what to do or where to go. She mouthed the word "bar" and I followed her over to the back of the club.

Amalia held up a fist full of cash and magically got the swamped bartender's attention. A tall lanky guy approached. His face was painted with white make-up and black contours on the bones. Around the eyes were bursts of color and what almost looked like a spider's webbing.

"What are you meant to be?" I called out to him as her poured Amalia a foamy plastic cup of beer.

"Dia de los muertos," he replied with a grin. Dia de los Muertos translated as "day of the dead" in Spanish.

"Awesome!" I called back, nodding my head in approval. "Can I get a rum and diet coke?"

He nodded and retrieved another plastic cup from underneath the bar.

"Diet coke?" Amalia chuckled.

"I'm trying to cut out soda altogether to make sure I fit into my dress."

"Fair enough," she mumbled through a mouth full of beer.

Amalia took a step to the side, smacking three party-goers with her wings. Just then I felt two warm hands wrap around my waist. I quickly turned around, half expecting some creep, but of course it was Alex.

"Your Grace," he joked, giving me a half bow.

"Do you realize how much you owe me for wearing this stupid wig?" I pointed to my head. "My scalp feels like there's a dead animal stuck to it."

"I know, my love," he leaned down and offered me a kiss. Then he pressed his lips close to my ear and whispered, "I'll let you pick the honeymoon destination."

I perked right up. "Are you serious? Wherever I want to go?"

He held both hands up, as if to surrender. "Anywhere you want to go, we will go."

I jumped up, careful not to hit anyone around me and Alex caught me mid-air. I wrapped my legs around his waist and grabbed his face in my hands.

"I fucken love you," I said right before kissing his perfect lips.

"I fucken love you too," he laughed and gently lowered me back to the floor.

"Where's Michael?" Amalia called over the loud music. Her question was directed at Alex, not to me and broke us out of our love trance.

"He's here," Alex scrunched his eyebrows. "He's just grabbing a drink. I'm sure he'll come find us."

Amalia scanned the room, taking large sips from her cup. My guess was she'd be drunk within the hour. She lowered her plastic cup and, with it, her jaw. I turned around to see what she was gaping at, and immediately spotted the problem. There was Michael, sans costume (he didn't even bother dressing up) walking toward us with someone I immediately recognized.

Long, dark hair, pink lipstick, chocolate-colored eyes, and strikingly beautiful.

Angela.

My eyes darted back and forth between Angela and Michael. They were standing close to each other, but the club was so crowded you didn't really have a choice. Angela was dressed as a sexy tiger. There wasn't very much to her costume. A black leotard, tights, striped animal ears, and a short tail pinned to her backside. Like Amalia, she too was wearing boots. The difference was Angela's went up to her thighs and had a four-inch heel on them. I turned my gaze back on Amalia, who looked as if she had just been punched in the stomach.

Michael finally saw her, and the two of them exchanged a long look. Her eyes scanned him from top to bottom, and then switched over to Angela, who was bopping her head to the music. Unaware of Amalia's death stare. Michael tapped Angela to get her attention. She flipped her dark-brown hair in a flirtatious swoop, but her expression fell quickly as soon as she saw Amalia. Angela gave me a small smile and I gestured a mini wave, out of forced politeness, pressing my lips in a straight line. She and I hadn't spoken since last year; she had just kind of fallen off everyone's radar. Of course she held a huge torch for Michael, and for a bit last year it seemed like he did for her. In the end, she didn't want anything serious and neither did he, so they stopped hooking up. But now here she was, in the flesh, ready to stir up some drama for Amalia, who, I noticed, just got a top-off from the bartender.

Angela whispered something into Michael's ear and then turned on her heel and trotted onto the dance floor. A moment later she was sandwiched in between two guys, both dressed like pirates. Michael made his way toward us through the sea of drunk twenty-somethings and stopped right in front of Amalia.

"Hey," he pulled her in for a weak hug. Alex gave my hand a light squeeze and I squeezed back. Being around Michael and Amalia made us feel closer to each other. Whatever problems we faced at least we were always on the same page emotionally.

Michael gently let go of Amalia, who still hadn't said a word, and reached over to give Alex a quick bro-hug. I cleared my throat and took a gulp of my drink.

"Hey Michael," I offered him a half-hearted smile.

"I like your costume," he said. "I see the two of you coordinated."

"It's a couple's thing," I shot back, hoping the words would resonate with Michael and show him how little he regarded his and Amalia's relationship. "I need to use the ladies' room. Amalia, care to join me?"

She nodded, her eyes fixed to the floor. I reached for her hand and led her through the crowd. Looking back, I saw Michael saying something to Alex, and Alex nod in agreement. My eyes then fell to Amalia. Her giant eyelashes were still holding up, but her blue eyes were red and glassy. She took another sip of her beer, and I could tell this would be one of her "black out" nights. I felt a wave of anger rush through me and realized I had been grinding my teeth. I genuinely hated the way Michael treated her. And a part of me was starting to resent her for letting herself constantly get pulled into this situation.

As soon as we made it to the bathroom, I noticed there was a line of nearly ten girls we'd have to wait behind. Too annoyed to care, I pushed open the door that said "men", and dragged Amalia inside with me. Locking the door, I took a deep breath and place my hands together under my chin as I gathered my thoughts on what exactly I was going to say to her.

Amalia crouched over the sink, her hands clasped on both sides of the basin. Rocking back and forth, I could have sworn she was going to throw up. Instead, she lowered her face into her hands and burst into tears.

I felt my shoulders sink and knew my lecture would have to be put on hold for another day. I watched her cry for a minute. Without a word, without any offerings, I just stood and watched my best friend come undone. She began to cry harder, her body shaking with each forceful sob. Amalia let out a long groan, followed by pushing herself up and feverishly banging on the door to one of the bathroom stalls. She kept hitting the flimsy door until her hands began to bruise, at which point she switched to kicking it with her boots.

I didn't know what to do. I wanted her to stop crying. I wanted her to stop freaking out. I wanted her to stop drinking all of the time, and I wanted her to stop dating Michael.

I just wanted her to *stop*.

I got it. She was upset, and rightfully so. Michael had ditched her for their museum date and, as far as I knew, this was the first time they were seeing each other outside of class in a couple of weeks. He still wouldn't commit to a serious relationship, and it was already October. I couldn't imagine being in her position.

Being so madly in love with someone and having that love be pervasively unrequited. The confusion, the pain, the anxiety. I really did understand going through all of that for someone you loved. For someone you believed you were meant to be with.

But this wasn't love, at least not on Michael's end. This was something wrong.

This was exploitation.

Finally, I darted over to Amalia and pinned her arms to her sides. She fought me a bit, still trying to break free and take her pain out on the door and walls. When she did calm down, her whole body relaxed. As she sobbed on my shoulder, I gently stroked her hair, coaxing her to calm down.

And through all of this I made a mental note to ask her where she got those fake eyelashes, because those suckers really held up!

"It's going to be okay," I whispered. She remained silent. Her sobs had stopped and she was left with wet, black streaks of make-up staining her cheek bones. I shook my head and continued to soothe her the best I could.

"You are stronger than this, Amalia, I promise," I muttered softly. "You just don't know it yet."

Fifteen – Amalia

"Just keep in mind finals are in three weeks," the TA for our class boomed out through a squeaky speaker. Feedback crackled through the antiquated sound system, and a few students flinched at the high-pitched noise. "I would suggest, as usual, to form a study group. Don't let this one slip through the cracks." As if any of us could forget for a single moment that the end of the semester was approaching. At least we had a couple of days off at the end of the month for Thanksgiving. He walked over to his laptop and dramatically shut the cover. "I hope you all found this review session helpful." He raised his eyebrows and waved us off. The two-hour review session was finally over.

The teacher's assistants were the worst. They were always doctoral students who had a giant stick up their ass. It was as if they went out of our way to scare us instead of doing what they were meant to do, which was to help and guide us. Being chosen for the position of TA was another part of the work-study programs here at NYU. A much better opportunity than the endless data analysis and mental torture I had to endure with Dr. Greenfield. I let out a deep sigh and made small circles on my temples with the tips of my fingers.

Michael sat to my right packing up his laptop in a new suede bag he had bought during a trip we took to Saks a few days ago. He had called me that Sunday morning, asking if I was free because he could use a "shopping buddy." Of course, I dropped what I was doing (which was watching old *Gossip Girl* episodes in my pajamas at two in the afternoon) and hailed a cab up to 5th avenue from my apartment in Murray Hill.

As I sat in the cab, I watched light snow flurries begin to fall over the city. Like a snow globe, everything looked so beautiful. That is, until all of this snow turns to slush. Dirty brown slush.

When I arrived at the department store, Michael was already there mulling over a few button-down shirts in the men's section. It had been a week since Halloween and this was the first time we had seen each other alone since then. I had seen him one time in between, in class, but school work was really piling up and we both had to concentrate hard on the lecture. There was no time to chat.

I ran my fingers through my curls, fluffing them up a bit to give them more of a bounce before we saw me. Coaxing the frizz into something manageable. My hair felt ice cold from the brutal temperatures and the snow. Even though it was only November, and technically still autumn, the temperature was still freezing. I closed my eyes and pictured Hayden in Florida. I wasn't sure when he was moving, but I was sure that I was envious of the warm, tropical sunshine he would be greeted with when he got there.

I took another step inside the well-lit store. Even from behind, I found Michael attractive. He stood perfectly straight, shoulders square, always an air of refinement about him. Wearing a dark- gray wool coat with midnight-blue-colored jeans, he pulled it off flaw-lessly as he ran his fingers over a cashmere sweater. I immediately regretted my choice in attire, a clunky purple sweater from H&M with a fake-leather jacket that fell right at my hips. As I looked around the store, I noticed most of the patrons were well-dressed. Women in dresses, even though it was freezing outside. Men in pea-coats or suits. Even the children were polished – in designer clothes. There were security guards at the doors decked out in three-piece suits in front of each entrance. It would never have occurred to me to get dressed up to go shopping, but I never would have guessed I'd be dating a guy like Michael.

I grabbed my compact mirror from my purse and applied a fresh coat of lip-gloss. An effort to look more presentable instead of like the chick that was going to try and nick something from the cosmetics department. Holding my head up, I crossed past two giggling teenage girls, who looked as if they had their own personal stylist, and tapped Michael on the shoulder. He greeted me warmly with a soft kiss. Instantly, I felt the sweet fuzzy feeling of desire splash around my heart, as if it was coursing its way through my emotionally starved body.

When he pulled away my body ached for more. I always ached for more. When it came to Michael, I'd never be sated

"Hi, beautiful," he purred in my ear. I closed my eyes and felt my shoulders relax. "Thanks for meeting me."

"Of course," I smiled. I was too grateful to be spending time with him to bring up what happened on Halloween.

After I had finished melting down in the bathroom that night, Olivia and I hailed a cab back to my apartment. She stayed the whole night to make sure I was okay, taking residence on my couch. She really was a wonderful friend. Her mothering affection gave me the inspiration to start planning her bridal shower. I thought it would be a good idea to have it during winter break. We'd all be too busy next semester, with graduation coming up, to be able to plan something. I was aiming for a day or two before New Year's Eve.

The slam of someone dropping their textbook on the floor knocked me out of my day-dream. Suddenly remembering I was still sitting in the classroom, not sorting through dress shirts.

"You okay?" Michael asked. He was standing over me, with a puzzled expression.

"Um, yeah," I scrambled to get my things together. "I have a couple of hours to kill. Do you want to get a cup of coffee?"

Michael reached out for my hand and pressed it to his lips.

I looked around and noticed everyone else had cleared out. Of course he wouldn't do something like that in front of others.

"I'm not sure I have the time," he frowned, as he let go of my hand to check his watch. "I want to spend as much time as I can studying for this exam." He gave me a half-smile.

"We can study together," I offered quickly. "Forget the coffee. Come back to my apartment and we'll have a study date like we used to do."

"I won't be able to concentrate," he leaned in close enough for me to smell his skin. Sandalwood, honey, and some other blend of intoxicating aromas. For a moment I closed my eyes, and I felt like the world had disappeared around me. I was so in love with him. I couldn't hold it in any longer.

"Michael," I whispered, his mouth inches from mine.

"Yes?" he breathed.

I kept my eyes closed as I let the words fall out of my mouth.

"I am so in love with you," I breathed.

I waited a beat and then opened my eyes to see that his were fixed on mine. He looked tired. He always looked tired. Like he had been born with less time to think than the rest of us, but with double the thoughts.

"Amalia," he said in a soft, low voice. "Are you sure?"

Surprised by his response, I answered as quickly as the words formed in my head.

"Of course I'm sure," I kept my gaze on him. His face paled, but I didn't turn away. I was studying him. Studying his eyes, his hair, his lips. Taking it all in, wanting this moment to freeze.

And for a moment there, I really believed he'd say it back. But, as always in my life, belief had inevitably set me up for disappointment. In reality, he didn't have to say anything. I just knew. I knew everything I felt for him, the love, the desire, and the desperation. I *knew* it was unrequited. And in that moment I let myself accept it. I genuinely accepted that I would love Michael, with all of my heart, but that he would never fully love me back. For a few precious moments, it didn't matter to me whether he loved me or not. All that mattered was that he was in my life. That I could share my life with his. That I could tie myself to him.

But you don't get to make that decision on your own. There's another part of the equation that has more say in whether you can stay in love. The other person. And in this case, Michael broke me out of my fantastical bubble.

My naive enchantment.

My self-less delusion.

"I'm not in love with you," he muttered.

As fast as my words had fallen out of my mouth and had lasted for a mere quarter of a second, his seemed to go on for a lifetime. Still staring into each other's eyes, I began to feel mine swell up. He placed his hand on top of mine and offered me as much solace as he could.

"But that doesn't mean I won't, or that I can't, be in love with you *someday*," his words sounding empty. "I mean, hell, we aren't even in a committed relationship yet."

"Why not?" I asked softly. I blinked back my tears and took a large gulp of air to help support my speech. "What are you waiting for?" I shrugged lightly.

"I honestly don't know," he uttered.

He sat down in the seat next to mine, still holding my hand but breaking eye contact. We both sat in silence, digesting what we had just said to each other. Silently assessing the damage.

"We've been together for months," was all I could muster up. "This is me, I have no tricks up my sleeve." I knew I looked desperate, but I was in need of an explanation.

"I know," he nodded. "I'm just not ready. I don't know, Amalia. There's just so much to consider. Finishing this program, for starters, getting into a doctoral program. I don't even know where I am going to be next year."

"Wait," I said, getting a little bit more of my strength back. "I thought you wanted to stay in New York. Are you applying to schools in other states too?"

"I'm considering it," he admitted, a grimace taking hold of his face

"What about your apartment?" I shook my head in disbelief. "Would you get rid of it? Sublet it?"

"I have no idea," he let go of my hand and sat back in the wooden chair. Our classroom was the size of an auditorium, I felt the space was fitting for this conversation. "These are all of the things on my mind right now. I feel incredibly overwhelmed."

I didn't know what to say. Anything I could think of just seemed to push him further away.

"If I stay with you, we might easily break up from the distance between us," he shook his head.

"Michael, we could break up for a number of reasons. But that's not what I want," I put my hand to my chest. "I want us to be together. I want us to be in a relationship. We'll deal with all of the other stuff when it comes up."

He looked at me and offered me a weak smile. "I don't want to hurt you." He touched my cheek, and I immediately leaned into it.

"Then don't," I pleaded, unable to hold back the tears any longer. "Please, just give us a fair shot. It's been years of this and I'm exhausted." I reached for his hand. "You don't have to be in love with me yet. But I don't know if I can continue down this path anymore without any kind of commitment. It's not fair to me."

"You're right," he said weakly, "It's not."

"Do you remember at Olivia and Alex's engagement party when you told me I had to make a choice?"

"I do," he whispered.

"Well, I can't believe I'm saying this," I started. "But you need to choose, Michael. Because I'm going to be honest with you, I fell apart when I saw you talking to Angela on Halloween."

"Why?" he raised an eyebrow.

"Because I have no idea whether or not you're sleeping with other people," I put up a hand before he could say anything. "And, honestly, I don't want to know. But I can't do it anymore. I am sick with anxiety." I over-enunciated the last three words, really trying to drive my point home.

"I had no idea you were feeling this way," he said. "I don't want to see you in pain."

I ran my fingers through my hair, thinking of the best way to say this.

"Look, you know how I feel about you," I shook my head. "You've always known."

He remained silent, softly stroking his index finger along my wrist. "I guess I have."

"And I know you have to think about it," I gently pulled my hand away from his. "Let's just both take some time, concentrate on Thanksgiving and preparing for our final exams. When that's all over, we should sit down and talk again."

I wanted him to tell me that he didn't need time to think. That he hadn't slept with anyone except me for as long as we'd been dating. I wanted more than anything for him to just be with me.

Honestly, how hard is it to just *be* with someone?

But he didn't say any of those things. Instead he bit his lip and nodded. I swear in that moment, I could hear my heart breaking.

"I think that's a good idea, Amalia."

"Okay, then," I gathered all of my strength and stood up. "I should go."

"We'll talk soon."

"Sure," I zipped up my jacket and stifled a sob as I turned away from him.

I opted for the stairs instead of the elevator, wanting to get out of the building as soon as humanly possible. I pushed my way through a crowd of undergrads, disgusted by their energy and enthusiasm. A few seconds later I was outside and felt the oppressively cold wind hit me. Not sure where to go, I stood still and replayed the conversation Michael and I just had over again in my head.

I felt like my life was falling apart. Cassandra and I weren't friends anymore and I missed her so much. Hayden was moving away to Florida and I'd probably never see him again. And I knew I should be happy about this, but selfishly, I knew Olivia would most likely drop off the radar as soon as she and Alex got married.

I had never felt so alone.

Sixteen – Olivia

"Pass the mash. Sweetie," my dad said to me after I scooped out nearly half the bowl for myself.

"What? I thought this was all mine!" I joked. Alex gave me a warm smile as I handed the serving- sized bowl to him to pass along to my father.

It was just the three of us that year for Thanksgiving. Alex and I rented a car and drove up to Rhode Island the night before in an attempt to beat the holiday traffic. The sweet scent of freshly baked piecrust carried through the house, along with the savory scent of the turkey my dad had just taken out of the oven.

"So, Alex," my dad dabbed his mouth with an ivory-colored cloth napkin. We usually ate with paper plates and Styrofoam cups, but I could tell my dad wanted to make a good impression for Alex's first visit. "How's school going for you?"

Alex swallowed his food and paused for a moment, thinking of how to form his answer. The fact was, Alex's grades were perfect. The lowest mark he had ever received in a class was an A-. My grades were pretty good too. I expected to get an overall GPA of three point seven. But compared to Alex's four, I might as well have been getting sent back to kindergarten.

"School is going very well, sir." He nodded.

"Oh, Alex, please don't call me sir." My dad laughed and held up his right hand. "You're going to be my son next year."

Alex and I exchanged a glance. "Okay, then," Alex hesitated before saying, "Dad."

My dad paled. "John's fine for now."

We all laughed. The smile on my face was so persistent my cheeks were beginning to hurt. The fire was roaring in the living room, but I could still feel the warmth from twenty feet away. Or maybe that was just the butterflies I got in my stomach whenever I was with Alex. Especially today of all days. We had never spent a holiday together with family, and it was very important to me that he and my father got along.

"The two of you are too quiet tonight. Come on! How's the wedding planning coming along?" my dad asked.

"It's coming!" I let out a throaty chuckle. I couldn't wait to be married, but planning the reception was giving me hives. "There's a lot to be done between planning the wedding, final exams, and applying for doctoral programs. But the wedding is a top priority. Although I don't even know why I'm planning to go to school for another four years because mom has suggested that after I marry Alex I should just live off his money and do nothing with my life."

"Well that certainly sounds like an idea," my dad said through chewing, "that your crazy mother would have."

Alex just rolled his eyes. "She's welcome to whatever I have or make. But I believe she deserves a life of her own as well."

I put my hand on his knee. "Don't worry sweetheart, I plan on getting into a far better doctoral program than you. Then, if you're good, I'll throw a little cash your way every now and then." I tore off a piece of bread and popped it in my mouth.

He touched his chin and pretended to ponder on this idea. "Will this be before or after you start paying off your exorbitant pile of student loans?"

I tore off another piece of bread and tossed it at his head.

"I worked really hard picking out that bread from the grocery story," my dad joked.

Alex leant over and kissed my forehead. I pretended to be offended and pulled away, all the while laughing.

"Back to the wedding. What's the name of the venue?" my dad leant in closer to the table. I had a mouth full of turkey, so Alex took the floor.

"It's called Mondrian," Alex paused to take a sip of his wine. "It's a beautiful hotel downtown in SoHo."

"Perfect!" my dad lit up. "I'll be able to stay at that hotel and get maximum time with my daughter on her big day." He let out a soft sigh. "I can't believe I'll be walking you down the aisle in less than a year."

Hearing my dad say that nearly brought me to tears. He had always been an amazing father, being there all throughout my childhood, supporting me both emotionally and financially through college. But now I was an adult I no longer expected that kind of assistance. Still, he was always there for me when I needed him. There was something even more special about how he was acting concerning the wedding. Something I was slowly learning was that if you really want to see how people feel about you, have a wedding. Everyone will show their true colors. From the best friend who would drop whatever she was doing to plan you a bridal shower, even in the middle of her own emotional crisis, to the mother who couldn't be bothered to offer any support, emotionally or financially, but was willing to sabotage it. Even Alex's father was on his best behavior since he found out his son was getting married. It warmed my heart to hear that the two of them were finally taking steps to repair their relationship.

"Do you know when your bridal shower is?" my dad asked, breaking me out of a daze.

I laugh and pushed some sweet potatoes around my plate. "Of course not! It's meant to be a surprise." My dad and Alex exchanged a knowing glance. "Wait. Do *you* know when it is?"

He and Alex exchanged another glance and Alex began to blush. Still laughing, I turned to Alex and grabbed his hand.

103

"Do you know when it is too?" My eyes were wide with antici-pation. I hated surprises. I especially hated it when everyone knew the details except me. "Did Amalia contact you?"

"No," he said in between laughs. "Why would she tell me when the shower is?"

"Exactly," my father chimed in, a wide grin spreading across his face. "Why would Amalia email us asking us what we thought about certain dates? Or wanting to make sure your registry was already set up at Crate and Barrel."

I cocked my head to the side and shook my head at them.

"Right," Alex waved his hands around. "I mean, it's not like we are going to show up at the end of it and help with bringing any presents home. I'm sure you can manage on the subway all by yourself with arms filled with gifts. I have faith in you, baby."

The two of them were downright giddy. I felt my eyes water from laughing so hard.

"Can you at least tell me what month it's going to be in?" I pleaded. It was obvious from their rapturous reactions that they knew all about my bridal shower. "Or maybe where it's going to be? I need to know how to dress!"

"How about this?" Alex looked at me and then darted his gaze back to my father. Calming down, my dad gave a small nod, smile still fixed to his face.

"It will most likely be before graduation," he offered.

I raised my eyebrows and gaped at him. "That's all you're going to tell me?"

"Afraid so, honey," my dad said while opening another bottle of wine. "And that's all you're going to get from us. So, who wants dessert?"

"I would love some dessert," Alex said in a joyful tone. I had honestly never seen him look happier.

"It is pumpkin pie?" I asked hopefully.

"With vanilla ice cream," my dad winked. He stood up from the table and made his way into the kitchen to retrieve the pie. I heard the fire crackling in the next room and closed my eyes for a moment, letting the warmth wash over me.

"Have I told you today how completely in love with you I am?" I push a stray hair back from Alex's forehead, his skin feeling remarkable soft to my fingertips.

"Thank you for the best Thanksgiving I have ever had," he uttered. He lightly ran his fingers over my cheek, stopping at my chin. Tilting my chin up for a kiss, I felt myself melt, as always.

"I'll never get tired of this," I whispered, as he slowly ended our kiss.

He took my left hand and helped it up higher. My engagement ring sparkled in the light, causing a tiny rainbow on the white tablecloth.

"Forever," he said in a voice so soft, I swear I could have died from happiness right then and there.

"Forever," I repeated.

We sat there for a few more moments, staring intently into each other's eyes. The rest of the world seemed to disappear. I realized, at that moment, that everything else was out of my hands. Out of my control. What Ph.D. program I got into for next year, or if I got into one at all. At that moment, I felt that I had everything I could ever want sitting right in front of me. Wrapped in a bow and perfectly delivered without a single blemish.

"You two love birds want more wine?" my dad asked, breaking us out of our trance.

"I'm fine with the pie," I smiled.

I watched my father serve us dessert, suddenly feeling like a little kid again. I couldn't stop smiling if I'd tried. Smiling at what would become, in time, a peerless memory.

It was officially the best Thanksgiving ever.

Seventeen – Amalia

"What was it that made you decide to apply for graduate school here a NYU?"

"Excuse me?" The question caught me by surprise, although it really shouldn't have. It was my third week into therapy and so far all we had talked about was my interest in furthering my career. It was getting to be a bit redundant.

"What were some of the deciding factors in choosing NYU?" Autumn tapped her pen against a legal pad. "As opposed to choosing any of the other programs you were accepted on?"

She wore her hair differently today, side-swept into a low pony-tail. Her usual pencil skirt was replaced with a pair of black dress pants. Still, she hardly wore any make-up and from where I was sitting, I couldn't see a single blemish on her porcelain skin. She was the type of girl whose sheer existence could upset you. I bet she felt very powerful in her pseudo-position of authority.

I look her straight in the eye and let out a long, exasperated sigh. "This was the best school I got into." It was the truth. I had only applied to a few other schools and, to me, NYU felt like the best choice.

"What other schools did you apply to?" she coaxed her red hair from one side of her neck to the other.

"Hunter College, Columbia University, and the New School," I answered impatiently. Every two minutes or so, I glanced at the clock that hung above her desk. The session still had half an hour left. I rubbed my forehead, trying to fight off a tension headache.

"So all the programs you applied to were in Manhattan?" she asked, narrowing her dark-green eyes.

"Yes," I answered curtly. "I wanted to live in the city. Is there a point to your line of questions?"

"How do you feel about living in the city now?" Her eyes back on her notepad.

Clearly there wasn't.

"I guess I feel the same way I have been feeling about it for the past two years."

"So, then you want to stay in New York?" she pressed on. "You wouldn't consider applying for Ph.D. programs or looking for jobs in another state?"

"I honestly don't know," I leaned back further into the plush chair. Final exams were a week away and all I could think of was how much time I was wasting here when I could be studying.

"Can we please talk about something else?" I pleaded.

"Okay, sure," She flipped the page on her yellow legal pad and scribbled down a few notes. Of course I wasn't privy to any of them. I was surprised at how easily I got her to agree to a change of topic. She flipped to a fresh page while I studied the seams of the withered carpeting beneath my feet. "I'd really like to hear more about your social life."

Here we go.

"What exactly do you want to know?" I asked with a fake smile.

"I want to know about your friends. How do you feel those relationships are going? And how about your romantic life? Are you dating anyone?"

I froze for a moment. The urge to brush her off was stronger than ever. But something else took over: the thought that I could actually vent to someone about my problems who wasn't directly in the middle of it all. Someone who could possibly see the situation for how it really was.

"Well, Autumn, I hope you have enough pages on your pad there because this story is not short."

She nodded, gesturing for me to continue.

I looked up to the ceiling and continued to stare at it while I unloaded onto her.

"When I first moved here, I had a best friend named Cassandra and a boyfriend named Nicholas. They were the two closest people in my life and I loved them both dearly. One day, Nick decided he no longer wanted to date me, basically because he was a selfish tool who only cared about things that could further his own career and cared very little about my interests. So he broke up with me a few days after my twenty-third birthday. A little while after that, I started hooking up with a close friend of mine, Michael. He was also a classmate and involved with another girl who lived in Arizona. But that didn't stop him from wanting to sleep with me. And even worse, it didn't stop *me* from sleeping with *him*. So that went on for a few months until I broke it off. I wanted more, and I knew he wasn't ready to leave his girlfriend. Flip to a couple of months later and Nicholas decided he would try to get back together with me. Which would have been great except at that point he had already turned into a pretentious douche bag. Still, I had loved him once. I thought maybe I could love him again. So we tried to move forward, but I broke it off a couple of months later. I couldn't stand the person he had become. Then in May of my twenty-third year on this planet, Michael showed up at my apartment, flowers in hand, the day before I was meant to leave for Brazil, a trip I had been planning all year. He asked me not to go on my trip, to stay and spend the summer with him while we "figured out" what was really between us. Basically he had broken up with his girlfriend, but things still would have been the same. No real relationship, no real commitment." I shrugged and glanced back to Autumn. "Shall I continue?"

"Please do," she said apprehensively, her eyes wide with attentiveness.

"So after I got home from Brazil, I had to stay with my friend Cassandra until I found a new apartment. You see, the lease was up and there was no reason to renew it with both of my room-mates moving out. I had to find a smaller, cheaper place to live." I suddenly wished I had remembered to bring a bottle of water with me. "But back to Cassie. My best friend in the whole world. The girl who taught me how to apply eyeliner when we were thir-teen years old and walk in high heels not long after. The girl who was always there for me, no matter what. Well, Autumn, the sad thing is, that girl is gone now. She has been replaced with some Manhattanite "glamazon" who treated me like a peasant for a year before I finally let her have it at my friend Olivia's engagement party. I haven't spoken to her since."

"Haven't spoken to Olivia since?" Autumn asked, her brows furrowed.

"No", I shook my head. "Cassandra. I ran into her a couple of time since then, but neither one of us made the first move."

"Who's Olivia?" she asked, edging closer to the end of her chair.

"She's my current best friend, beating out Cassandra for defending champion. I'm her designated maid of honor," I paused for a moment as I thought about how to describe Olivia. "She's a really good person. She helped me get back on my feet and find the apartment I currently live in. Oh, and she also goes to school with me at NYU."

Autumn took a deep breath, writing as fast as she could. She stopped every couple of seconds to shake out her hand. Her pen had to be running out of ink at this point.

I sat patiently while she caught up.

She finally stopped writing, composed herself, and then asked, "Did you date anyone else after Michael?"

This was the part of my story I was dreading the most. The part where I hurt Hayden.

"I did," I uttered, picking at the hem of my shirt. I was silent for a few moments. Memories that had been long tucked away

109

came flooding back to me. How he kissed, how he smelled. How he loved me.

"Hayden," I said in a low, soft voice. "He's a really great guy. But I ended things with him too."

"Okay, wait a minute. Then what happened?" she challenged. "If he was so great, why would you end things with him?"

"Because I always kept coming back to Michael," I answered plainly. "Hayden and I weren't in a committed relationship either. Despite the fact that we were seeing each other for months." I pressed my lips into a flat line as I felt the all-too-familiar sting of tears trying to push their way out of my eyes. "And it was my doing. I always kept him at a distance."

"Because of Michael?" she asked in a tone that was unusually gentle for her.

I nodded as I quickly wiped my fingers underneath my eyes so she could tell I was tearing up.

"And now you're pretty much caught up," I let out a throaty laugh. "Michael and I are seeing each other again now, but it's not without its complications."

"Such as?" she put the legal paper aside, and for a moment I felt like I was talking to a friend.

Still, this was not an easy conversation to have. Not with anybody. I glanced at the clock and felt a wave of relief as I realized we only had two more minutes of time left.

"Well, the main issue is commitment. I told him I wanted us to take the next step, to be seeing each other exclusively," I tapped my fingers on the arms of the plush chair. "I want him to treat our relationship with the respect it deserves and start working with me toward a future for us together." I once again shrugged my shoulders, as if I was talking about someone else. As if it wasn't painful for me to relive the feeling of him telling me he wasn't in love with me.

Or the feeling of remembering Hayden telling me he was.

I anxiously twirled a strand of blonde hair through my fingers.

"So I told him to take some time to think about what he wanted."

"And what is it that you want, Amalia?" she crossed her arms and cocked her head to the side.

I paused for another moment. It was so quiet in the room, I could hear the sound of her watch ticking on her wrist. My eyes fell to the floor as the words fell out of my mouth.

"I want him," I muttered, forcing a small smile.

"Why?" she asked.

"What?" I started looking around the room.

"Why do you want to be with someone so badly who doesn't feel the same way about you?" she pressed on.

I glanced back over to the clock. We had gone over by a minute. I breathed a sigh of relief and stood up.

"Our time's up," I said flatly. I stood up and smoothed out my clothes. "And I have to go home and study for finals."

Autumn stood up and followed me to the door.

"Amalia," she started. "When we meet next week, I want an answer to my question. I want to know why you want to be with Michael."

"Sure," I muttered. "I'll have some charts made up for you."

I didn't turn around to look at her. She'd heard enough about my private life for one day. Without another word, I turned on my heel and walked out of her office.

A few weeks later I began my annual journey back to Staten Island to spend some quality time with my parents. And by quality time I meant me traveling for an hour to see them, and my parents probably not even noticing I was there. Or worse, my father would have a freshly printed test for me to give to Michael. I shuddered at the idea.

The good part about this visit was that Aaron would be home from college. It had been months since we'd seen one another, and we had a lot of catching up to do. He reached out to me last night and we exchanged a few texts when he got back to my parent's house from Syracuse. He was "home" for a week for his winter break. Technically, my parent's house, not his dorm, was still his permanent residence. Classes ended yesterday morning for NYU with the collection of our final exams. I had reached an odd point with my feelings about school. Normally I would drive myself crazy about my work. I'd be worrying about my grades, staying up until all hours of the night studying, and subtly asking every other student how they did on their exams so I could compare grades. But I didn't feel the usual anxiety this time. Instead, I studied as hard as I could for two weeks before the test, even getting together with Olivia a couple of times for a study session. When the night before the exams came, I went over my notes as much as I could before calling it an early night and going to sleep at ten o'clock.

To get downtown to the ferry I took the subway down to Whitehall Street. When I exited I noticed Battery Park in the not-so-far distance. Despite how cold it was, and the fact that it was three o'clock in the afternoon, there were plenty of people swarming the area. I wondered why none of these people were at work.

I glanced at my cell phone to make note of the date. December 23rd, the day before Christmas Eve. Dropping it back in my purse, I felt my face fall. My parents don't celebrate any holidays, but Aaron and I decided that we would get each other both a little something, just to feel like we were a part of what everyone else in America was a part of. Or, at least, that's how it seemed.

I boarded the ferry to Staten Island and promptly walked to the outside area, knocking into no less than four people in the process. I leaned my arms over the railing, flinching at how cold the steel was. We began moving shortly after and the breeze gliding over the New York Bay blew my hair into my face, trapping loose strands of blonde in my lip-gloss. I reached into my purse again, this time retrieving a hair tie, and quickly threw my hair into a messy bun. The moment I did, I thought about how much my mother would hate to see my hair like this. I smiled.

112

As I stared out into the water, passing the Statue of Liberty on the way, I let my mind wonder about Michael. I had seen him yesterday in class, but we had exchanged only brief pleasantries. He seemed downcast, but I chalked it up to him just being tired. We were giving each other space while he thought about whether or not he was ready to commit to me exclusively and start treating this thing we had as a legitimate relationship. Yet still, as absorbed as I was by my thoughts of Michael, it didn't stop me from wondering about Hayden. I knew I'd reach out to him on Christmas some way. Either by text or phone call, I wanted to wish him a happy holiday.

Would I always be this way? Would I always spend my time wondering about what could have been with either one of these guys? Or could I get to a point where all of my energy and thoughts were focused on just one of them?

Michael was spending Christmas with his family. I didn't expect to hear too much from him while he was there, and I didn't want to be the one to contact him during his "thinking" time. Every moment of my life was fettered by Michael's decisions.

Through the speaker someone announced that we were docking. I made my way to the front of the boat, eager to get back onto dry land. As usual, Aaron had volunteered to pick me up from the terminal. I walked with the crowd of people onward toward the exit and spotted my brother right away. He was holding two cups of coffee in his hands and I immediately let out a chuckle.

"It's so good to see you!" I wrapped my arms around my brother's torso as he held the coffee tightly, careful not to spill any on us. "And thank you for the coffee." He looked older than the last time I had seen him. His blonde hair had darkened slightly with age, and I could have sworn he had grown an inch or two.

"I figured you could use all the energy you can get," he said as we headed to the parking lot. "You know, for dealing with mom and dad."

"You got that right," I muttered. "I see you're picking me up in *my* car again?"

He laughed and helped me with my overnight bag. "Come on, it just sits there while you're in the city!"

A ten-minute car ride later, we were pulling into my parents' driveway. I heard the front door open in sync with my car door closing. Aaron shot me a look, followed by a bright smile. I rolled my eyes and let out a throaty laugh. At least I wasn't alone in thinking my parents were a little odd.

"Hey, kiddo," my dad was the first to greet me. He gave me a quick hug in the doorway.

"You're letting all of the cold air in!" my mom hollered from the kitchen.

"She's right," he said, motioning toward the couch. "Take a load off."

Aaron and I shed our heavy down coats and placed them next to us on the couch. My mom finally emerged from the kitchen. She had an apron tied around her waist and patches of flour on her hands and cheeks. Her blonde hair was in a loose ponytail and she was hardly wearing any make-up. Unusual for her.

"Um, hi mom," I gave her a small wave. "Are you baking something?"

"Cookies," she answered. "For you and your brother."

"We're very grateful," Aaron uttered in a sarcastic voice. My dad raised his eyebrows at him as if to say, "Watch it."

"So, Amalia," my mother chimed in, rubbing her hands on her apron. "You didn't have time to do your hair today?"

Knew it.

I took a deep breath and untied my hair from the bun and shook it out. "Is this better?"

"Sure," she shrugged. "Although I do like it better when you blow your hair out straight."

"I know you do," I closed my eyes for a moment. I had been there less than five minutes and they were already getting on my nerves. How was I going to make it through two days here?

"Are you still with that boy, Amalia?" My dad asked. "Holden?"

114

My heart sank. No one had asked me about Hayden for a long time. Apart from my therapist, Lauren Autumn Mercer (what a bullshit name). I slowly shook my head and folded my arms across my chest, suddenly feeling like I needed them to keep me from falling apart.

"No," I stammered but quickly caught myself. I didn't want my mother to get a whiff of any weakness in my voice. "We broke up nearly a year ago."

Had it really been that long? These past few months with Michael seemed to have flown by, and through the entirety of it I never really seemed to get my footing.

"Anyone else in your life?" he asked with a smile. I could tell immediately where he was going with this.

"No one who I'd feel comfortable enough proctoring an exam for," I winked.

My dad and his test. For some reason, Aaron never had the treat of the test being administered on any of his girlfriends. But then again, Aaron never told our parents when he was dating someone. He never outwardly lied; they just never actually asked.

"Are you sure, Amalia?" My dad walked over to his printer. "Because I've actually taken the liberty of adding a few more questions. Topical ones, nothing too invasive." He reached down and pulled out what looked like no less than ten freshly printed pages.

I raised my eyebrows, hoping my facial expression would do all of the talking for me.

"I can always email it to you," he offered. He put the papers down on the computer desk and shrugged. He did seem a bit embarrassed, and for a moment I actually felt like what he was trying to do was find a way to bond with me. I looked him over. Short dirty-blonde hair, nearly the same color as my mom's (gosh, come to think of it, the four of us probably looked like the *Children of the Corn*), a worn-in Mets t-shirt and light-colored jeans. No shoes. I remembered how he would always walk to the mailbox

115

with just his socks on, and my mom would give him hell for it. The poor guy.

"You know what, Dad," I gave him a half-smile. "My purse is really full right now, but how about you email it to me?"

"Really?" he perked up like I had just told him he had won and all-expenses-paid trip to Cabo. "Is your email still the same? Ms.CutieAmalia@aol.com?"

Aaron burst out laughing and I felt my ears grow red with embarrassment. "No, I haven't had that email address since high school, Dad."

I was lying. I totally still had that email address. I never used it; it was completely embarrassing. But it was part of my youth that I want to remember. No matter how old, or how cultured I became, I wanted to remember that I was the skater girl with torn jeans and Vans sneakers who owned that email address.

"Her email address is Hastings.A@NYU.edu," my brother provided.

"Got it," my dad quickly jotted it down on a loose piece of paper on his desk. "I'll email it to you when you go back home to Manhattan."

Home to *Manhattan*? I still felt as if this house was my true home, but it had been a long time since I had spent any real time living here. I nodded, catching Aaron's eye in the process. He could tell what I was feeling, because he was begging to feel it too.

One day you're living in your house, the same house you've always lived in. Then one day you've grown up, and it's not your house anymore. It's your parent's house. It's scary how fast that day comes, even if you've gradually been feeling it over a span of years.

Ernest Hemingway wrote in his novel *The Sun Also Rises* about how his character went bankrupt. "Two ways. Gradually, then suddenly." It was the same way I felt about growing up. There were two elements to it. It was a slow, painful process that seemed to last a lifetime. And then the rest of it came all at once. As I looked around my parent's house, a house that had not been redecorated ever, right down to the frayed beige carpet beneath my socks, I realized that I was in the *suddenly* stage of growing up.

Trying to push down the sting of nostalgia, I walked over the fridge. Hoping for something to calm my thoughts, I scanned the items and my eyes landed on a bottle of white wine.

"Are you saving this for something?" I asked my mom.

"Not really," she shook her head.

"Mind if I open it?"

"It's only four o'clock in the afternoon," she answered, a displeased look on her face.

"Is that a yes or a no?" I asked, exasperated by her tone.

"Go ahead, Amalia. If you want to start drinking in the middle of the afternoon, who am I to stop you?"

"Cool," I muttered. "Aaron, you want some?"

He walked over to me and silently poured himself a glass. My mom took off her apron and tossed it on the counter. As she walked out of the kitchen, she shot me some serious side-eye.

I looked at him and raised an eyebrow. "It's good to be home, bro."

He raised his glass at me and then took a generous sip. "It's going to be okay."

"Yeah," I muttered. I took another sip of Riesling before answering with, "That's what everyone keeps telling me."

A few hours later, Aaron and I were hanging out in his bedroom. We took turns telling stories of what had happened to us since the last time we had seen each other. He told me about his girlfriend: a nice girl from Minnesota with red hair. Her name was Claire, and Aaron told me he was already in love with her.

"How long have you been dating?" I asked. I was sitting on Aaron's computer chair while he lounged on his bed. The blue paint that enfolded the room made me feel a pang of nostalgia. I hadn't even dared to go into my old bedroom yet.

"Four months," he answered. "I met her on campus when she

was lost. I noticed this beautiful girl with a puzzled look on her face and a scrunched-up map in her hand. So I walked up to her and offered my assistance. We talked for a few minutes before I asked her to have dinner with me the next night. We've been together ever since." The glow coming from him as he talked about Claire was undeniable. There was no question in my mind; he was definitely in love.

"I'm really happy for you," I said. "Can I offer you just one piece of advice?"

"Sure."

"Don't ever take your relationship for granted. Recognize that being in love is special and that not everybody gets to feel that way in their life. If you truly love her, you need to work through the problems the two of you encounter. You can't just walk out one day and bail on the relationship. Trust me, you'll regret it."

"Are you speaking from experience?" Aaron asked quietly?

"I don't know," I raised an eyebrow. "What I do know is that I have never seen you look so happy."

"And I don't think I've ever seen you look more miserable," he countered. His eyes offered a comfort I hadn't received from anyone in a long time. "What's going on with you? Have you and Cassandra managed to patch things up yet?"

I shook my head. "I don't think that's going to happen."

"Why?"

I paused for a moment, thinking about my answer. "Because, I don't think she wants to try to be friends again. And worse, I'm not sure I want to either." I turned my gaze to the floor. "I don't like the person she's become. I feel like if I met her now, without having being friends with her in the past, we wouldn't like each other."

Aaron leaned over and offered a supportive hand on my shoulder.

"It's okay," I muttered. "Some people show up early, playing a major role in your story and then exit. Some people you'll meet later on, and they'll stick it out with you till the end."

Aaron nodded and patted me on the back for good measure. I sighed, wondering who else in my life was finishing out their role, and who was going to be there until the end. And then I wondered something worse.

I wondered if I had any control over it at all.

Eighteen – Olivia

I had gotten a phone call early Saturday morning from Amalia asking me to meet her for lunch at Sweet Revenge, a cute place known for its rustic appearance and artisan cupcakes. With no plans of my own, I happily agreed. Alex was out this morning for a jog and then heading to Trader Joe's for some food shopping. How he could possibly stand to jog in thirty-degree weather was beyond me, but I figured it meant I had the bathroom all to myself, so I didn't question it.

With only two days left in the year, I could honestly say I was looking forward to a fresh one. This would be the year I would graduate with my Master's degree. This would be the year I would be getting married! I hummed around my apartment, filled with happiness and ease. I was nearly finished with all of my doctoral program applications and we had all taken our final exams last week. School wouldn't resume again until the beginning of February. A whole month off from school. I resolved to finish what little what left of my applications and commit the rest of month of January to wedding planning.

At around eleven-thirty I took the overhead tram into Manhattan and then hailed a cab down to the West Village. As I turned the corner onto Carmine Street I saw Amalia standing outside waiting for me. I shivered at the harsh wind, curious as to why she'd be waiting outside in this weather. She was wearing a cream- colored coat that I have never seen before. I couldn't tell what her outfit underneath looked like, but I saw from the bottom half that she had on black tights and high heels. Her blonde hair was down and curly again. Her make-up was minimal, apart from some black eyeliner on her lower lash line. She was starting to look like herself again. She was standing on the sidewalk with her hands in her pockets, shivering slightly.

"Hey!" I called to her from ten feet away. I waved a gloved hand and her face lit up when she saw me.

"How's your morning been?" she took her hands out of her pockets and began rubbing them together.

"Good," I answered with a shrug. "Having a lazy day."

"Your hair is getting so long," she said out of nowhere. She reached for a strand of my hair and I teasingly swatted her away.

"Growing it out for the wedding," I took my gloves off and ran my fingers through my extra-long, brown hair. At this point, it fell straight down to the middle of my back. "I figure I'll have more options for what I want to do with it at a longer length."

"Speaking of your wedding," she said in a sing-song voice. "Have you picked out your bridesmaids' dresses?" She reached for the door handle and pulled it open slightly.

"I'm thinking something in the lime-green family? Or the brightest pink I can find."

"You're hilarious," she muttered. "Either way, we have to go to this place called Vanity Projects to get our nails done the day before. Their salon is supposed to be the best in the city!"

"One step at a time!" I laughed.

We walked through the front door, but the whole place was empty.

"Are you sure they're open?" I looked around for an hours-of-operation sign.

A moment later, a chorus of people yelled "Surprise!" and I screamed. Clutching my chest with one hand, I lightly swatted

121

Amalia with my other one. One after another, the guests let go of their pink and purple balloons, allowing them to fly freely up to the ceiling.

Once my heart rate had returned to a normal speed I looked around the room, taking in my surroundings. There were glass towers on all of the tables holding about ten cupcakes each. In addition to the sweets, each place setting was already set with a salad and a wine glass. Just as I was about to open my mouth to comment, Amalia handed me a flute of champagne.

"In case you haven't figured it out, this is your bridal shower."

"I can see that," I uttered, feeling my eyes tear up from joy. I was so touched that she went through so much trouble to do this.

"I can't believe you thought through this entire thing yourself!" I said, still standing in utter disbelief.

"Well, I can't take all of the credit," she replied. "Your dad actually did a lot of the work. He supplied me with the phone numbers and addresses of the women in your family. He also paid to rent out this place. We have it all to ourselves for three hours."

My dad was nowhere to be seen. He probably felt it best to show up at the end and help with the gifts. There was a pile of them on a small table next to a chair. Traditionally, the bride sits down in front of her guests and opens all of her gifts while her maid of honor writes down who gave what – making it easier to send out thank-you cards later on. Everyone ooh's and ah's at the Corningware dishes, the Lenox silverware, or the lingerie from that one aunt who always acts just a little crazy.

Amalia squeezed my arm lightly and then motioned toward the back of the room. There, in a fitted blazer, pearls around her neck, and high heels on her feet, sat my mother. She was nursing a glass of champagne and was looking around the room. No one was sitting next to her and I felt a pang of sadness for her. I put the champagne flute down on a neighboring table and crossed over to my mom.

"Hi, Mom," I said softly. I slowly pulled out the chair next to her and sat down. "I'm surprised to see you here."

"Why would you be surprised to see your own mother at your bridal shower?" she asked, an edge to her voice.

Of course she wasn't going to make this easy.

I pursed my lips together and shook my head. "That's a good question, Mom." She lowered her head and I reached for her hand. I let out a long, exasperated sigh. "Why are you acting like this? Are you really so unhappy that I'm getting married?"

"No," she met my gaze. "I am honestly feeling like you've grown up to be this amazing person, and I can't take a single ounce of credit for it."

Stunned at her honesty, I was unsure of what to do. Should I offer her a hug? Lie, and say she did have a part in it? Or did we both accept that this is the truth, that she hadn't been a part of my life in quite some time now.

"Mom," I started, unsure of where I was going with this. "I know we haven't been in each other's lives very much lately. But if you're open to it, I would really like to remedy that."

"How?" she asked. It was a good question. How do you just erase years of problems? Arguments? Or even worse, silence?

"I know we can't change what has been done," I answered. "But I would really like to try to move forward with you. Maybe we can start by you helping me out with some of my wedding planning?"

"I didn't realize you needed any help," she raised an eyebrow. "You seem so well put together."

I laughed so hard my eyes started to water. "Mom, I am drowning over here. Between schoolwork, the move into Alex's apartment, planning the wedding, and planning for my future, I can hardly remember what day it is. Of course I need help!" I folded my hands and placed them on my lap. "And I'd be lying if I said that picture of Alex hugging that girl hasn't been in the back of my mind ever since you showed it to me. I am not well put-together, I am hanging on by a thread."

"I'm sorry, Olivia. I honestly didn't mean to start trouble for the two of you. I think the best thing to do would be to directly ask him about it. Get it over and done with so you can focus on other things. And just so you know, the gown you picked to be married in is very beautiful."

"Thank you," I gave her hand a little squeeze. "And if you're not too busy in the up-coming weeks, maybe you can help me get a handle on the seating chart!"

"Of course," she smiled.

I heard the door open and watched as a few more guests arrived. Family members I hadn't seen in years, and never would have expected to make the trip out to New York.

"I had better go make the rounds," I said. "I am really glad you came, Mom."

"I am too," she said, tears forming in her eyes.

I turned on my heel and headed toward the front of the restaurant, where Amalia was standing, tossing a roll of toilet paper up and down.

"What is that for?" I asked, following the toilet paper roll with my eyes.

"It's for later, when we wrap you up in it," she laughed.

"Like a mummy?"

"Duh! No, like a bride."

"I have no idea what you're talking about," I laughed.

Amalia dropped the toilet paper roll onto the table and wrapped her arms about me. "Seriously, Olivia, it's a good thing you made me your maid of honor! What would you do without me?"

I returned the hug, swaying her tiny frame back and forth.

I sighed heavily as I looked around the room at this wonderful gathering she had prepared for me.

"I honestly have no idea."

Nineteen – Amalia

"We took our final exams for the first semester a couple of days after I saw you last," I said to Autumn.

The day after Olivia's bridal shower, I attended my last therapy session until school picked back up in February. I was happy to throw the shower for her and she really seemed to love it. But I did feel a sadness while I was there with her. It felt like Olivia has always been one step ahead of me in life. Maybe I should be talking to Autumn about this instead of school, which was always our primary topic of conversations.

"How do you think you did?" She had a pensive look on her face.

I took a deep breath and thought for a second. "I actually think I did pretty well. Despite all of the stress I had this semester, I still managed to get all of my work in on time and study as hard as I could for every exam."

"What do you think your GPA will be?"

"I am hoping for a three point five," I said. "I may be a tad optimistic to think that way, but fingers crossed!"

She let out a small laugh and it surprised me. It was the first time she offered me a smile that wasn't laced with smugness. I couldn't help but notice how straight her teeth were. Momentarily self-conscious about my own appearance, I pulled my navy-blue cardigan a little tighter around my chest.

"Amalia," she pulled her chair a bit closer to mine. "Is it okay that I sit over here?"

"That's fine," I replied with apprehension, not really sure where this was going.

"I want you to know that I am not here to judge you. My methods may seem a bit too firm at times, but truly I am here for your support."

"I appreciate that, Autumn. But as I said when we began therapy, I didn't choose to be here. Dr. Greenfield forced my hand."

"And how do you feel about therapy now?"

I paused for a moment. It was an interesting question because our last two sessions weren't as dreadful as the first few.

"I can say I feel a little better about it," I said. "But I still don't love the idea of spilling all of my private life to someone I hardly know."

She offered me a smile and an understanding nod.

"Amalia," she began. "Last week when I asked you what it was that you loved about Michael, why you wanted to be with him so badly, it was because the two of you seem to have a very unstable relationship with one another."

"That's not true," I snapped. Immediately feeling defensive of both myself and Michael.

"From what you've told me, you began this relationship in secret. He had a girlfriend at the time. You put your relationship with Hayden in jeopardy too when you slept with Michael. And now that the two of you are both free to be together, he doesn't seem too committed to your relationship. I just don't see how it could work."

I sat there stunned. The way she laid out the details of our time together for me, it sounded horrible. Worse yet, it sounded incredibly juvenile.

"Look, I know it might seem like I am chasing after someone who will never be with me. And I'll admit, sometimes it does feel that way to me. Having said that, I do love Michael. I love how smart he is, how he's always challenging me. I love his refined demeanor and how incredibly adult he is compared to most other guys my age. I love that he has goals for his life and he stops at nothing to achieve them. Even if it means–" I drifted off.

"Even if it means you'll never truly be a priority in his life?" she challenged.

I shook my head defiantly. "No, you're wrong. I am a priority in his life."

"Amalia, I am not saying this to anger you. But, think about it, why hasn't he fully committed to you yet?"

"He's not ready," I replied. Plain and simple. "He and I will be together once he's ready. There's a lot to consider, neither of us knows where we are going to be next year."

"You mean in terms of school?" she asked.

"Yes."

"But haven't you all applied to programs in the New York area?"

"We have," I answered. "But Michael has also applied to a few others out of state."

"I see," she said, a grimace on her face. "You need to make sure you're making the right decisions for yourself."

Who else would I be making them for?

For someone who was supposed to remain neutral and composed, she sure had no problem letting me know how much she disliked my decisions. I checked the clock. Ten more minutes of this and I'd be free from her until next semester.

"Honestly, I'm exhausted," I said, my shoulders sinking. "I just finished finals week and threw my friend Olivia a bridal shower a couple of days ago. What I need is to go home and take a nap." I began to collect my things, not caring that we were meant to continue for ten more minutes. "I am going home, Autumn. I will see you in the beginning of February. I hope you have a good New Year's Eve."

Before she could answer, I turned on my heel and darted out of her office.

Twenty – Olivia

For New Year's Eve, we all decided to skip the parties and the bars and just get together at my and Alex's apartment for some drinks. I had spent the day making appetizers for the group, and baking cookies to go with them. I was really surprised that Alex didn't put up more of a fight when I suggested staying in for the holiday. He would usually rant and rave about how we'd be "missing out" on all New York has to offer by staying in. But even he agreed we were too wiped out from finals and wedding planning to spend the night at some overpriced club.

At around nine-thirty, I poured myself a glass of red wine, the champagne chilling in the fridge for later.

"You look very pretty," Alex had snuck up behind me and slid his arms around my waist. A warm rush of blood surrounded my heart. Two years and I still got butterflies from him.

"Thank you," I turned around to face him. Standing on my toes, I offered him a kiss. A small sigh escaped my lips as he cupped my face in his hands. His lips barely touching mine, I whispered, "It's easy to pull off a little black dress in twenty-degree weather when you don't have to leave your home."

"Well you definitely pull it off," he took a step back. His eyes scanned me from top to bottom and I could feel myself blush. He took both of my hands, whispering, "And later, I'm going to pull it off." I drew in a quick breath and bit my lip. Looking up at him through my eyelashes, I pulled on his arms to draw him in closer.

As soon as I leaned in to kiss him, my mother's words popped into my mind. I knew I had to ask him now.

"Alex," I started. I need to ask you about something."

His brow furrowed as he considered my words. "From the look on your face, this doesn't seem like it's going to go well."

"That's really up to you," I countered.

I took a deep breath and spat it out.

"A few months ago, my mother showed me a picture of you hugging a girl with long red hair." I tried to gauge how Alex was feeling by his reaction. But he had none. "We've been together long enough for me to know all of your friends. So I guess what I'm asking is, who was that girl?"

As if on cue, there was a knock on our door. Alex looked at me with a blank expression on his face. I raised an eyebrow, indicating that I would make whoever was at the door wait a minute for the truth.

Alex didn't seem to care or notice. Turning on his heel, he reached for the door. For now we would have to shelve this discussion. We had guests to tend to.

Amalia was the first to arrive. Her hair was blown out straight again and it looked very blonde next to her shiny silver dress. The hem stopped just above her knees, so although the dress was very form-fitting, it wasn't too short. Her eyes were rimmed with black eye-liner, and her lips were painted a glossy pink. No tights (she must have been freezing outside!), and black high heels. I was sure her sexy look was for Michael, who had already told Alex he was running a bit late.

"Hey!" she handed me a bottle of Prosecco as she stepped into the entry way. "You both look nice."

"Thanks," I said, handing the Prosecco off to Alex. I managed to avoid eye contact with him as his fingers brushed against mine. "So, did you hear anything about any of our grades yet?"

Amalia's face paled. "Why would you put this in my head on a holiday?"

"I haven't gotten any of mine either!" I quickly tried to put her at ease. "But that's it, no more school talk. I promise." I gave her an over-the-top nod and pretended to zip my lips.

She nodded back. "I am pretty sure I heard Dr. Greenfield mumble something about the grades needing to be submitted no later than January twelfth." She shrugged her tiny shoulders. "So I wouldn't start driving yourself crazy for another week."

"I'm not driving myself crazy," I said. Alex shot me a look and then exchanged a knowing glance with Amalia. "What? I'm not!"

"Its fine, baby. This is what we love about you," Alex hugged me from behind.

"I'm going to be a bit anxious until we get out grades back," I uttered, easing out of the hug. "It's the last transcript that doctoral programs are really going to care about."

"We know," they both said in unison.

"Hastings, you want a cookie?" Alex held the tray out under her nose.

"Absolutely," she grabbed two and started nibbling away.

Good, I didn't burn them.

"Why don't you put on some music, baby?" Alex took a cookie off the tray and devoured it in one bite.

"Good idea," I brushed past him and turned on the playlist on my iPod I had made for this occasion. A Sia song came on first and I adjusted the volume, keeping the music at a low, conversational, level.

Amalia crossed past us and walked over to the windows in our living room. We had a great view of the Manhattan skyline from our apartment in Roosevelt Island. Amalia stood in awe, taking it all in, as the moonlight bounced off the water and lit up the sky. Every skyscraper stood tall and proud. Taking a few steps toward her, I smiled. Watching her see what I experience every day out of my own window made me realize I took it for granted. I watched her eyes studying Manhattan, transfixed on a city she had grown up next to and still managed to be affected by to this day. A city that she stared at through my floor-to-ceiling windows. As if seeing it for the first time she had ever laid eyes on it solidified what I already knew to be true.

I loved living in New York. There was no way I was ever moving.

A couple of hours later, Michael graced us with his presence. Alex opened the door and I twisted around to get a look at Michael. He was wearing his usual dark-denim jeans, paired with a button-down with a grey V-neck sweater over it. The Michael uniform. Alex had on black slacks and a checker-patterned button-down. He had his sleeves rolled up, showing his forearm. I always found that sexy about him. But right now sex was the last thing on my mind.

Amalia shifted her weight and sat up a little straighter once she heard Michael's voice. I turned to face her, us both sitting on the couch, and gently took the glass of wine from her hand. Surprisingly, it was only her second drink of the night. A puzzled look crossed her face as I placed the wine glass on the mahogany coffee table, but she didn't fight me on it.

"Michael's here," I said pointlessly. The music was still low enough that I could hear them talking. I craned my neck a bit to see if Michael was going to walk this way, but he and Alex were talking about the Giants game that was on this week. I pressed my lips in a straight line as I watched Michael talk. He hadn't even bothered to come talk to Amalia yet. Turning my attention back to Amalia, I saw she was staring at the same thing I was, only she had a longing look in her eyes. Leaning in a bit closer to her, I placed a sympathetic hand on her shoulder. "I want you to do something for me tonight."

"What's that?" she gave me a weary smile.

"I want you to relax and just be yourself."

"What do you mean?" Amalia let out a soft chuckle. She smoothed her hair down and then ran her fingers along a wrinkle

131

that had formed on her dress from sitting.

"I mean all this," I motioned up and down to her. She scrunched up her face and pursed her lips. "You are beautiful, Amalia. You are smart, you are funny, and above all you're a good person. I know that might not seem like much of a compliment, but believe me it is. Especially when you live in a city like New York. You have been through so much these past two years, and you're still standing. You're still applying yourself and you're still open to taking a chance on love. And don't get me wrong, I find that very admirable." I paused for a moment, thinking of how exactly I wanted to phrase my next sentence. "I know you love Michael." She lowered her head for a moment and then quickly raised it back up. I could tell this conversation was making her uncomfortable. "And I know how badly you want him to love you back. But *this* is not you."

"What's not me?" she asked, shifting her weight again on the couch. She tucked a strand of blonde behind her ear.

I noticed the guys were wrapping up what they were talking about, so I lowered my voice.

"This," I touched her stick-straight hair. "And this," I motioned at her sparkly dress. "And most of all, this." I pointed at her face. I was probably being a little more firm with her than I had to be, but she had to get this through her head.

"I don't know what you're talking about," she countered. "I blew my hair out straight, what's the big deal? And I wear make-up every day of my life." She glanced over at her wine glass, probably hoping she could get it back without me swatting her hand.

"You only wear *this* much make-up when you are planning on seeing Michael. Same thing with the hair. It just comes across like you're trying to be a different person entirely."

Her face growing red, she darted her eyes to the floor and then back up to me. I could tell she was feeling self-conscious, and I was beginning to feel like the bad guy.

"And that's not to say you don't look beautiful. Amalia, you're a pretty girl and you're going to look pretty no matter how you do your hair and make-up. Or if you're wearing jeans and converse sneakers or a tight metallic dress." I was talking fast, quickly trying to get to the point of my rant. "What I'm trying to say is that you shouldn't have to try this hard to look good for someone. Michael knows you, he knows how you usually dress. And if you feel like you have to go through some kind of make-over transformation to get him to notice you, then I can't imagine he's making you feel good about yourself."

"It's not like he asks me to straighten my hair and wear shiny lip-gloss," she shrugged, a pained look on her face. She crossed one leg over the other and tugged at her hemline.

"Then why do it?" I asked, trying not to sound judgmental. "It just seems so out of character for you."

She paused for a moment and seemed to consider this. She shrugged lightly and sighed.

"Because I want to look perfect," she stated.

I pursed my lips, thinking of what I should say next. Before I could say another word, Alex and Michael joined us in the living room, taking a seat on the other couch. Amalia's eyes were fixed on the television. Some New Year's Eve special was playing, but I could tell she wasn't really watching it. Michael scanned Amalia up and down. I guess this dress *was* on his approved list of outfits.

A low buzzing sound came from the coffee table and Amalia immediately reached for her phone.

I took a sip of my wine and inched closer to see who had texted her.

"What the hell?" she mumbled. Her brows furrowed and a puzzled expression told hold of her face.

"What is it?" I asked, the four of us looking at her for an answer.

She let out a soft snicker. "Cassandra just texted me."

"What did she say?" Michael asked

Amalia's eyes widened and then darted to Michael. I think we were both surprised that he showed interest in what was going on in her life.

Another point I had been trying to make.

Amalia shook her head. "Nothing, really. All she wrote was *Happy New Year's Eve*."

"Are you going to write back to her?" Michael asked.

Again, Amalia seemed genuinely surprised that he was asking these questions.

"I don't know if you should," I chimed in. "Maybe it's best just to get her out of your life altogether. She's become pretty toxic."

Amalia nodded, but her downcast glance told me she wasn't going to take my advice. I looked over to Alex, who hadn't said a word in the past ten minutes. He just sat there next to Michael, watching the mess that was Michael and Amalia unfold.

"I'm just going to write her back the same thing she said to me," she said without looking up.

"Who wants more wine?" I stood up, playing hostess in an attempt to thaw this icy situation.

"Me," the three of them all said at once.

"Coming right up," I collected their wine glasses. "Alex, care to join me in the kitchen?"

"You bet," he stood up and followed me out of the living-room area.

"What do you think they're talking about?" he whispered. Never one to relish relationship gossip, I was surprised to hear these words come from his mouth.

"I think I know what they're talking about," I said, reaching in the cupboard for another bottle of Malbec.

Alex raised an eyebrow "So, tell me." The volume of his voice made Michael and Amalia both stop talking and raise their heads to look at us.

I cocked my head to the side and gave him a look.

"Sorry," he whispered.

A beat later Amalia stood up. Michael instinctively put his arms on the back of the sofa, sprawling out. How nice it must be to remain so calm and cavalier while the person you're dating is suffering from daily mental breakdowns because of you.

"Hey," she uttered. "Can I talk to you alone for a minute?"

I expected her eyes to be watering, or at least be wearing a downcast look. Instead her eyes looked wide and hopeful, with a smile tugging at the corners of her lips.

"Steal her if you must," Alex said with a dramatic sigh. He crossed past us and joined Michael in the living room, their eyes both fixed on the television.

"Let's talk in my bedroom." She nodded and followed me out.

She glided into my room and kicked off her high heels. After a quick scan of the bedroom, she darted for our queen-sized bed and immediately plopped down on it. I followed suit and sat down next to her.

"So what's going on?" I asked. "Did Cassandra say something else to you?"

"Nope," she refocused her weight on the bed, tucking her legs and bare feet underneath her. She gave me a big smile and I could tell by the glassy look in her eyes that she had downed the rest of her wine when I wasn't looking.

"Okay then," I smoothed out my black dress. I was feeling slightly annoyed at her behavior. I had to admit, Amalia had grown up a bit since I first met her, but she still had a little ways to go. Chiding her about her drinking wouldn't get me anywhere right now, so I just let it go. I tucked it away, and reminded myself to talk to her about it at a better time. "If it's not Cassandra that's made you so happy, then that could only mean one thing." I could feel my face twist into a grimace.

Amalia pulled her weight up, balancing on her knees as she grabbed me for a hug. Her curtain of blonde hair ensconced my face. As I returned the hug, I breathed in her scent. Whatever perfume she was wearing was being masked by the amount of alcohol she had drunk. I loosened her from the hug and coughed.

"Michael and I just had a talk," she beamed.

I folded my hands and placed them on my lap. "Amalia, you were only alone with him for five minutes. How much could you have discussed?"

"A lot," she slurred. A wide grin spread across her face and she widened her blue eyes. She put her hands on my shoulders and looked deep into my eyes. "We're going to do it."

"Do what?" I asked, but I had a pretty good idea of what she was talking about. I just hoped, for her sake, it wasn't true.

"We're going to give it a real shot," she answered. My hope deflated. "He told me he thought about the deadline I had given him–"

"The ultimatum," I cut her off.

"Yup, that," she continued. "And he decided he wants us to date exclusively and see where this relationship can take us!"

"So that's means, what, like you're boyfriend and girlfriend?" I shook my head, puzzled by this entire encounter.

"That's exactly what it means." Her eyes reached a new circumference of wide.

So many thoughts came flooding to me at once. "But what about Hayden? Are you sure you're completely over him? And what about applying for doctoral programs? Has Michael decided if he is even going to stay in New York? Are *you*? I mean seriously, Amalia, what's your plan?"

She looked at me, her head cocked to the side, a knowing smile on her face. "This was my plan, Olivia."

"What are you talking about?" I inched back, suddenly worried her craziness might rub off on me.

"Being with Michael," she went on. "This has always been my plan. School, work, all of the other stuff will fall into place. I can work harder, I can beg professors for letters of recommendation, but I could never *make* Michael want to be with me. And now he does. The big challenge is over. From here on out, it's a cake walk."

I gaped at her. She sounded absolutely unhinged. "Amalia, I still think you need to–"

136

Shaking her head, she put a hand up, indicating me to stop talking. She dropped her bare feet to the floor and picked up her shoes. With a stroke of one hand she smoothed down her hair, and reached for the doorknob with the other.

"There's nothing left to worry about, Olivia." She offered me a warm smile. I couldn't tell if she was acting like this because she was drunk or not. "You and Alex, me and Michael. This is how it's supposed to be." She said the words slowly, letting each of them land for effect. I sat perfectly still, frozen in place on my bed. She slid her shoes back on and then looked back at me. I took a deep breath. I wanted to say something to her, to tell her she was making a mistake, but I just couldn't find the right words to say it.

"We're going to leave now," she uttered. "Michael and I really just need to spend some time alone."

"Okay," I mumbled.

"I love you. Have a happy New Year," she said, pretending to tip a hat towards me.

"Yeah. You too." I stayed where I was, too unnerved to see her out.

She twisted the doorknob and then offered me her last words of the night.

"Don't worry, Olivia," she raised an eyebrow. "Everything is going to be alright."

And with a turn of her heel, she exited my bedroom, gently closing the door behind her.

Twenty-one – Olivia

I woke up to the sound of fresh coffee percolating in the kitchen. Which was, in my opinion, the best sound to wake up to. And the best scent. Rolling over on to my side sent a pain shooting up my back. As I gingerly tossed the duvet off my waist, I felt a dull pain in my head. Confused by the body aches, I rubbed my eyes and then remembered what had happen.

New Year's Eve, too much champagne, passive aggression, and the worst part of it all, Michael and Amalia were in an exclusive relationship. They were "officially" dating; a certificate should be presented at any moment.

Actually that wasn't the worst part of the night. The worst part of the night was when I told Alex to sleep on the couch.

Sitting up in the bed, I pulled my arms up to stretch. That's when I realized I was still wearing the little black dress I had on last night. Taking in a deep yawn, I reluctantly put my feet on the hardwood floor. The sound of the coffee machine stopped and I sighed. I had to go in the other room and force Alex to tell me what was going on with that girl. The girl with the red hair.

A moment later I was measuredly gliding into the kitchen in one of Alex's NYU t-shirts and a pair of yoga pants. Before I could even open my mouth to yawn, he handed me a cup of coffee, followed by two pills. I raised an eyebrow.

"Ibuprofen," he said with a shrug. "It should help with the hangover."

"And how do you know I'm hungover?" I responded, my voice flat.

He swept a strand of messy brown hair off my forehead. "Because I'm hungover." Taking my hand, he led me to the living-room sofa. "And I've got about sixty pounds on you."

Letting out a deep sigh, I plopped down on the couch and took a much-needed sip of coffee.

Alex and I exchanged glances and he smiled. Even first thing in the morning he looked good. His dark-blonde hair was tousled ever so slightly: a look most men would probably put product in their hair to achieve. Still in his pajamas, Alex was wearing a plain-white undershirt paired with black and grey flannel pajama pants. He took my left hand (the one what wasn't holding on to the coffee for dear life) and kissed it ever so gently. Right by where my engagement ring was.

Even when I sleep, I never take it off.

"Alex," I murmured. "You're sober, you're awake," I looked him square in the eyes. "And you're stalling."

Alex let out a soft chuckle. "No I'm not, sweetheart."

"Then at the risk of sounding redundant, who the hell is that girl?" I was growing more and more impatient.

"If you're talking about who I think you're talking about, the woman with the red hair is my cousin, Lauren."

"So, your cousin has been here in New York all of this time and you didn't think it was worth mentioning?" I narrowed my eyes.

"She doesn't live here in New York," he started to explain. "She lives in New Jersey with her boyfriend. She's in the doctoral program here at NYU, but I hardly ever see her. Her schedule makes ours look empty."

"That explains why I've never met her," I offered. I could feel my defenses coming down. "But not why you never told me about it."

"With everything that's been going on it honestly just slipped

139

my mind," Alex took a step closer to me and I fixed my eyes to a spot on the floor. "You'll definitely get to meet her at the wedding."

Softening, I took his hands in mine. "That's right, it's a new year," I said through a grin. "This is the year we're getting married."

"I had that same thought when I woke up," he offered me another kiss and I let out a small sigh. "Don't you have another fitting coming up?"

He was right, the day after tomorrow I had an appointment at Wedding Atelier on Madison Avenue to try on the first adjustments to my gown. I smiled at the thought of getting to put on my wedding dress again, all while praying they didn't somehow alter the dress into just a pile of tulle and lace.

After taking a few more sips of my freshly ground coffee, I sighed and shook my head.

"What is it?" he asked, a slight chuckle to his voice.

"I have something else on my mind, apart from the wedding dress."

"What's that?"

I opened my eyes wider and pursed my lips. "You know what it is," I narrowed my eyes in a playful way and scooted a bit closer to him. "Can we just talk about what happened last night for a second?"

"Ah. I know what this is about," he replied with a nod. "You're referring to our dear friends Michael and Amalia,"

"You didn't see her face, babe. I mean, I guess I could chalk it up to her being drunk, but the look in her eyes was just so *unhinged*."

"What exactly did she say to you?" a brief look of curiosity claimed his face.

"She said something about how everything was going to be okay now." I squinted as I tried to remember her exact words. Four glasses of champagne wasn't helping my memory any. "That all she really ever wanted was Michael to commit to her." I reached for my mug on the coffee table and took a long sip. Stifling a yawn, I continued. "And as I'm saying it out loud it doesn't sound all that crazy. You just had to have seen it, I guess, for it to really make sense."

Alex furrowed his brows and leaned in to the plush back of the sofa. A lazy smile spread across his lips and I could tell that even though it was nearly noon, he was still much too tired to talk about this. He wrapped an arm around me and gently pulled on me until my head was on his chest. I took a deep breath in, and nearly forgot what we were even talking about. I lifted my head ever so lightly and he rewarded me with a soft kiss.

"Here's an idea," he whispered, his face nuzzled into my hair. "As you pointed out earlier, today is the start of a new year. So how about from this day on we let our friends take care of their relationship drama."

"I just worry about her," I mumbled back.

"I know you do, and that's what makes you such a good friend," Alex sat up a little straighter and looked in my eyes. "And I can't believe I am going to say this," he took a deep breath and slowly released it. "But I am a little worried about her myself."

This took me completely by surprise.

"I thought you didn't like her?" I questioned with a smirk.

Alex gave me a slight eye roll before reaching for his mug. "She's your best friend, Olivia. I know I used to give her a hard time and I'm not saying I'll be inviting her over for tea and biscuits anytime soon," he said with a shrug. "Having said that, I don't think what Michael's doing is fair to her." He took a sip of his coffee and I nodded. He looked as if he wasn't sure what else to say.

"Maybe you can talk to him about it?" I asked, with an air of hope.

Alex considered for a moment but shook his head. "That's not really something I'd be comfortable talking to him about."

"I thought you two were really close?"

He took a beat and glanced out of the window into the city across the water. I felt a smile tug at my lips as I joined him in soaking up the beautiful view of the Manhattan skyline from our apartment on Roosevelt Island. He broke his gaze and turned back to me, bending down a bit so I could put my arms around him. I was still facing the window.

"Olivia," he started. "I don't think anyone can get *close* to Michael."

My eyes remained fixed on the black and white town I had grown to love. I thought about Alex's suggestion, to stay out of Amalia's drama. I wondered if it was possible. But there was one thing that was undeniably true.

"I think you're right, sweetheart." Raising an eyebrow, I could feel the weight of Alex's stare. "Michael doesn't let anyone get close to him." I stood up on my toes to be face to face with Alex.

"And I don't think he ever will."

Twenty-two – Amalia

"Do you want coffee?" Michael called from his kitchen. I pictured him staring at the clock above the television until enough time had passed for him to push down on his French roast.

"Is that even a question?" I let out a small laugh. I was tangled in the sheets, and my outfit was a messy pile on the bedroom floor. Grabbing some pajama pants off the side of his bed, I realized I felt pretty good in spite of how much I had to drink last night. After putting on the last article of clothing, I strutted into the kitchen with a new air of confidence.

I was more than ready to have breakfast with my new boyfriend.

Michael had woken up about an hour before me and was already showered and dressed. But since he had nowhere to go, he hadn't bothered with one of his usual, perfectly coordinated, outfits. Wearing jeans and a blue sweatshirt that read "Columbia Alumni", I realized that underneath all of that refinement was a more casual guy. One who felt comfortable enough to leave his hair undone and his button-down shirts in the closet. On the other hand, he might just be too exhausted from partying to bother with his appearance.

After we left Alex's apartment last night, we came back to Michael's place to crash. When we got here, a part of me wanted to start talking about our new relationship immediately. I was so happy, I could barely keep the words to myself. But as soon as we made it inside he started kissing me, leaving me both speechless and euphoric.

I walked gingerly over to the bistro table and slowly sat down, careful not to trip on Michael's pajama pants that were dragged on the floor. A carafe of coffee had already been placed on the table, along with two tall mugs. Watching as Michael flipped a perfectly fluffy pancake, I poured myself a much-needed cup of coffee. I couldn't help but sigh as he finished preparing the meal and stacked the golden-brown cakes on top of one another.

Lowering my head into my hands, I let out a small sound as my alcohol-induced headache started to get a little worse.

"How do you feel?" Michael materialized in front of me. He was holding a bottle of water and some pills.

I pulled my curls into a tight ponytail, tying them up with the hair tie I always had on my wrist.

"Physically?" I gave him a weak smile. "I feel pretty awful."

"Here," he said, handing me the pills. "These will help."

I studied the pills on the table while I opened my water bottle. "What are they?"

Pulling out the chair across from me, Michael offered me a small smile. "Those two are aspirin, the other one is a vitamin."

I swallowed the pills and then used my fork to stab a pancake from the stack. Biting into it was sweet relief on my grumbling stomach. At least I didn't have the usual nausea that accompanied my hangovers.

"How are you feeling?" I asked, pouring some extra maple syrup on my food for good measure.

Michael swallowed an oversized piece of pancake and nodded. "I feel fine. A bit of a headache but it's going away." He looked up at me and smiled. "Plus, I didn't drink as much as you did." He lifted up the coffee mug and gave me a small toast.

I felt a little nervous about the next topic I was getting ready to bring up. After a two-second mental pep talk, I finally got the nerve to ask him about what was really on my mind.

"So," I lazily swirled the spoon in my coffee, unable to meet his eyes. "How are you feeling about what we decided on last night?"

I could feel Michael's gaze sharply switch from his food over to me.

"I'm feeling good about it," he offered. But that was all he said.

Too scared to ask him to elaborate, I merely nodded as a million thoughts fluttered through my mind.

Where was this going? Would we still be together after school ended? How would we make it work if he ended up in a Ph.D. program across the country?

The anxious thoughts weren't helping my headache any, so I tried my best to keep them out of my mind. At least for today.

For right now all I could do was enjoy the ride and hope, more than anything, that it all worked out.

I got back to my apartment that day at around four-thirty and shuffled quickly into my building just as the sun was going down. The seasons in New York could be awfully depressing. Freezing winters, hardly any sunshine, inflating subway prices, not to mention the sheer isolation. When the holidays were over and it was still twenty degrees outside, it was hard not to feel depression. Even under the best circumstances.

Like getting to have breakfast with your new boyfriend.

Turning the key in my front door, the memory of my former roommates came back to me. I imagined I was back in my old apartment in the West Village and Christina was sitting by the coffee table, biting into an apple (she always ate so healthily). The sunlight would flood into the sitting room and she and I would trade stories about our days. Cassandra would inevitably show up at my front door, scratching the floors with her high heels. We'd chat over a bottle of pinot about Michael and how badly I wanted to be with him.

Liz would be nowhere to be seen.

Sitting in my apartment now, filled with furniture and clutter but empty of memories, just made me realize everything I had lost over the years. I missed our group study sessions. I missed the novelty of starting something new. I even missed Christina a bit.

I missed Cassandra *a lot*.

Sure, I finally had Michael, whatever that meant. But I missed feeling like things were possible. The cushion of knowing I had a few years to figure out what I was going to do when I graduated from NYU. I ran my fingers through my hair and hung my head. Maybe I was more hung over than I thought.

The fact of the matter was that I had no idea what I was going to do when I finished my graduate program. The idea of going through more school once excited me. But, at this point, I was merely exhausted by all of the work and pressure. I didn't know what was the right thing to do.

A beat later there was a knock at my door. I jumped up and opened it – not a smart move without asking who was there first. Olivia stood in the doorway wearing fuzzy white ear muffs and holding two to-go cups of coffee.

I wondered if she knew how ridiculous she looked.

"Hey," I said, motioning to the couch I had just been moping on. "What are you doing here?"

"I was in the neighborhood."

"Liar," I laughed. "Come on in"

She looked around my apartment. The first thing I saw her eyes catch was the sink full of dishes. The second was the blanket balled up on the couch that I had just been sulking on.

"Happy New Year, my friend," I muttered sarcastically.

"What's going on?" she cocked her head to the side.

"Just perseverating about my future," I answered, reaching for one of the coffees. "Or lack thereof." I grimaced before taking a sip of what turned out to be a vanilla latte.

"With Michael?" Olivia ran a finger over my counter top, almost examining my living quarters.

I shook my head. "No. I feel like he and I are finally on the same page." Whether or not that was completely true, I wasn't sure. But I was happy enough with him willing to commit to me to stop picking at it. I shook my blonde hair out of a messy ponytail, letting the curls hit my shoulders. "I'm worried about the other parts of my future."

I knew I was being evasive, but I honestly didn't know what to say. All of pathways I once saw as choices were now twisting into traps.

"I thought you said everything would be fine now that you're with Michael," she paused to sip her coffee. "He's all you've ever wanted."

"This coffee is really good," I offered her a fake smile, hoping to change the subject. "Where is it from?"

"Stumptown on 8th street," she turned on her heel and lazily dropped herself next to me. "Now, back to what we were talking about."

"Anyone ever tell you that you're too smart for your own good?" I teased. She wasn't having it, though. Her furrowed brow told me she was all business.

"I told Alex I wasn't going to get involved with your love life anymore, but I care too much not to."

I let out a long sigh. "Well, Michael may be all I've *wanted*, but that doesn't mean I still don't *need* things for my life." I rubbed my forehead. "Like a job lined up for after I finish this program."

"What do you mean?" she asked. "Aren't you applying for doctoral programs?"

"I am," I answered quickly. "But what if I don't get in."

"Come on, Amalia. You have to have a more positive attitude!"

"I don't think my *attitude* will sway the admissions committee in any way." I offered her a small smile, but I could feel my eyes fall to the floor. "They can't see me here, kvetching about it."

There was something else, something bigger than my fear of not getting in to a post-graduate program. I hadn't considered this before but somehow it was right there on the tip of my tongue.

"What if I don't want to get in?" I raised my eyes to meet her gaze. "What if I don't want to do this anymore?"

I thought of telling her that the thought of five or six more years in school was downright daunting. But I really didn't want a lecture right now.

Slowly rubbing my temples, I awaited her response. With her lips pressed into a straight line, Olivia looked like I had just told her I was going to jump off the Manhattan Bridge.

"What are you talking about?" her voice rising an octave. "This is what we do. College, graduate school, and then post-grad. It's the only way to get the jobs we've always wanted." Her eyes were wide, commanding attention.

I considered what she said for a moment. "And what is the job that you have always wanted?"

"I want to do research," she shrugged as if she was ordering extra fries. "Alex and I both do. And hopefully we'll be fortunate enough to teach some classes also." She squinted her eyes at me and raised one furrowed brow. "You are still planning on sending out your applications, right?"

I let out an exasperated sigh as the idea of four more years in school stabbed its way through my chest.

"I am nearly finished," I rubbed my eyes. This conversation was exhausting me. "If I can just get a decent letter of recommendation for Dr. Greenfield then I am done." I hoped this was enough of an explanation for her to drop the subject. From the look on her face, I could see that it was not.

"What's wrong, Olivia?" I asked in an exasperated tone.

"I am really surprised by how you're acting," she said flatly. "I thought we were all on the same page."

"What page is that?" I asked, trying to keep the bite out of my voice. I felt like Olivia was constantly challenging every move I made. Consistently making me second-guess myself.

"The one we were all on when we met. The one where we

148

finished out NYU, and then went on–"

"And then went on to spend another ninety thousand dollars on a doctoral program?" I spat out. "I just don't know how much longer I can live like this?"

"Live like what?" Olivia threw her hands in the air and started pacing.

"Look, Olivia," I stood up and made a point of keeping my voice in a measured tone. "I already have loans on top of loans. NYU is not cheap." I ran my fingers through the ends of my hair, not sure how to say this without her feeling insulted. "You are marrying Alex. You told me a while back that he doesn't have any loans to pay back, that he paid as he went through college and graduate school." Her face scrunched up as she realized what I was getting at. "He'll help you." Shrugging, I let out a soft sigh. "When you're married, he'll help you pay off all of your loans."

Olivia pursed her lips. I could tell we were teetering on the edge of a fight. Bound to fall into a battle if one of us didn't choose our words carefully.

"Okay," she started. "I understand where you're coming from." Her face un-scrunched and a look of hope washed over it. "You know you can defer paying your loans for as long as you're in school. That means if you get into a program here you won't have to pay the loans back while you're in school."

I shook my head. "Even if I do that, they'll still be accumulating a lot of interest."

Olivia's eyes dropped to the floor. I could tell she didn't know what to say.

I sprang up from the couch and crossed over to grab a bottle of water from the fridge. Tossing one to Olivia, I put on my best "I'm fine" face. She didn't want to talk about this anymore and neither did I.

"On to happier subjects," I forced a toothy smile. "I've been cooking up some ideas for your bachelorette party!"

Quickly, Olivia's tense stance relaxed. Letting out a soft chuckle, she took a step forward and then joined me on the couch.

"What did you have in mind?" she raised an eyebrow. "Oh, and the next word out of your mouth better not be–"

"Strippers?" I cut her off. Blushing, she gently swatted my knee. "Exactly, Amalia. No strippers."

I put my up hands in mock defeat. "As you wish, princess." It felt good to talk about this. Planning a party wasn't stressful. At least not compared to mapping out your entire future. "How about dinner, destination to be determined, followed by celebratory drinks at the Bubble Lounge?"

The Bubble Lounge was a landmark champagne bar downtown in the TriBeca neighborhood.

Olivia pressed her lips together and shook her head. "It closed a few months back."

I made what sounded like a mix between a sigh and a laugh. "Of course it closed." I looked straight at Olivia and shook my head. "Is it just me, or are all of the great places closing?"

"It's different for you, being a native New Yorker," she offered. "Don't let it get you down, Amalia. There are still a million fun things to do here." She put her hands on my shoulders. "Still a million different ways to get in trouble!"

"I'll figure out something epic for us to do," I said softly. "Your singleness is going to go out with a bang."

Twenty-three – Olivia

Thanks to the alarm clock not going off on my phone that morning, I was already late to my first class. I was darting down 5th avenue, making a beeline straight for Washington Square Park. I was only on 5th avenue and 16th street. I still had a little while to go.

"Olivia?" a voice called from behind me. My first instinct was to ignore it. I was already late and chatting with someone right now would only make it worse.

"Olivia Davis?" this guy wouldn't give up. I stop talking and whipped around, stunned by who was standing in front of me.

"Hayden?" I stood still and offered him a smile. I breathed heavily a few times, trying to catch my breath after my sprint.

"Hey, Olivia. How have you been?" He folded his arms across his chest and I followed suit. It couldn't have been warmer than thirty degrees outside.

"Busy," I let out a breath. "How about you?"

"Same," he let out a chuckle. "I am only going to be here for a few more months and then I am moving to Gainesville."

"Our old college town?"

"That's the one."

Amalia told me once that Hayden and I went to the same college for undergrad. I still, to this day, couldn't place him. Then again, I did party a lot in college.

"So you're definitely moving, then?" I asked, hoping he couldn't hear my disappointment.

"I am," he pressed in lips in a straight line, shuffling his feet underneath him. "Did Amalia mention it to you?"

I nodded. "She did. And I know things are weird between the two of you right now, but I also know she's not happy with you moving a thousand miles away."

Hayden's face looked tired as he offered me a defeated shrug. I figured if I was going to do something it was now or never.

"She still cares about you," I blurted out. "And she misses you."

Hayden gaped as soon as the words hit the cold winter air. He slowly nodded and said, "I am very happy to hear that she does." His eyes looked a little glassy, but I assumed it was from the wind. "But she is in love with someone else. I have no right to make her feel guilty or to make her believe she should get me to change my mind and stay here. Even though I would." He paused for a moment and then looked up again. "I would stay here if she asked me to. Even though I don't want to live here anymore."

Hayden's words broke my heart a little as they fell, crushed and hopeless, from him mouth.

"Can you do something for me?" I took a deep breath. "I have no right to ask you to do anything, you hardly known me."

Hayden raised an eyebrow.

"Could you try to see Amalia one last time before you move? Just for a quick cup of coffee, even?" I offered my friendliest smile.

Hayden's eyes dropped again as he considered this, but finally he answered.

"I'll reach out to her and see if she wants to meet up," he shrugged.

"Thank you, Hayden." I glanced at the time on my phone and inhaled sharply.

"Is everything alright?" he asked as I shoved my phone back into my purse.

"I am just really late for class." I turned around and started walking as fast as I could. "Thank you again!" I called back.

Twenty-four – Amalia

I just woke up to realize that it was Sunday morning and my weekend was nearly over. Michael and I had gone out to yet another fancy restaurant last night. The place was beautiful and the food was fantastic. But the restaurants were always dark and loud. We hardly had a chance to talk while we were out.

I definitely wasn't complaining about being taken out to dinner, I just was so tired from school work that I would have relished the opportunity for him and I to just stay in.

Everyone in the city was always moving, even in the frigid month of February. And everyone I knew was more than ready to brag about which hot spot they went to the night before. I remember when going to Coney Island for a hot dog was a big deal. These days you had to be *seen*. Seen out at the right places, with the right people. Drinking the right drinks and wearing the right shoes. Over the last five or so years, the New York social scene had become not only exhausting but impracticable.

I lay in bed with my eyes closed, wondering if Michael had ever stayed in on a Saturday night before and just ordered a pizza.

Rolling on my side, I saw he was already awake and typing something on his phone.

"Texting your other girlfriend?" I asked through a yawn. It was the first time I had referred to myself as his girlfriend. I wasn't sure he noticed.

"Ah, you're awake," he put his phone down on his night stand and then climbed on top of me.

"Omph! I've only been awake for thirty seconds." I repositioned myself so he wasn't crushing me.

"But you look so cute in the morning," he chuckled.

"I doubt that," I let out a throaty reply. "I need some coffee."

"Amalia, you always need coffee."

I looked at him, relaxing my tense muscles as he brushed a strand of hair away from my eyes. His dark hair was definitely a mess, but I didn't care. Before I could say another word, his soft lips touched mine. He wrapped an arm around my waist and pulled me tighter to him. I kissed him back slowly at first, unlocking all of his flavors. His hands ran down my back, pulling at my pajamas with a real feeling of urgency. As his hands cupped my face, I had completely forgotten why I was protesting this just a moment ago. He clearly wasn't bothered by my lack of make-up, my frizzy curls, or even me not having brushed my teeth yet. I mustered up my energy and playfully pushed Michael on his back while I jumped on top of him. With one clean motion he easily yanked off my shirt and then moved on to pull off his. Laughing, I fell back down in the pile of sheets and blankets.

I had a feeling my Sunday was going to be a lot more fun than expected.

A few days later I walked up to Dr. Greenfield's office, fully prepared to ask him for a letter of recommendation for the doctoral programs I was applying to. It was getting late in the year to send in your applications and if I didn't have everything in by the end of March, no admission department would even see them.

I curled my fingers into a small fist and gently knocked on his door. A second later the door swung back and I nearly fell over my feet. August was walking out just as I was walking in. And from the expression on his face, I could tell his meeting had not gone well. I opened my mouth to say hi to him, but he just pushed past me and darted for the elevator.

"Come in, Miss Hastings," Greenfield mumbled and I smoothed out a few wrinkles on my shirt.

I cleared my throat and sat down on the small brown chair that faced his desk. His office hadn't changed at all since the last time I had been in here. Still very bleak, lots of books, and one framed picture of a woman that I still couldn't get a good look at.

He began slowly pacing back and forth across the small room.

"What can I do for you?" he asked in his southern drawl.

Nervously, I held up the forms in my hand and gave him my friendliest smile. "I was hoping you would be able to write me a faculty letter of recommendation for the programs I am applying to for next fall."

He stared at me blankly, not taking the forms out of my hand. I lowered my eyes and carefully slid them onto his desk, hoping he didn't take my hand off in the process.

"And which programs would that be?" he stopped pacing and slid the forms toward him but still refusing to look at them.

I tried my best to steady my voice. The last thing I wanted was to sound like I was babbling.

"I am applying to Hunter College, the New School, the program here at NYU–"

He put up a hand and I quickly stopped talking. Narrowing his eyes, he thumbed through the forms I had placed on his desk. I pressed my lips into a fine line as I waited for him to start speaking again.

"Amalia," he let out a sigh and lowered himself into his leather chair. "I have no problem writing you a letter of recommendation."

I could feel my mouth fall open as soon as those words were spoken.

"So," I nervously started picking at my shirt. "You'll help me?"

Dr. Greenfield leaned back in his chair, crossed his legs, and put his hands into the steeple position.

"Let me ask you this question, miss. Why do you want to apply for a doctoral program here in New York?"

The question caught me off guard because the answer was so simple.

"The next step in finding a job in my field requires a doctorate," I shrugged. "And I only applied to schools here in New York because—"

"Because it's safe?" Greenfield questioned.

"I'm sorry," I cocked my head to the side. "I don't follow."

"Have you done much traveling within the States? Or Europe, perhaps?"

"I've gone on a few family vacations when I was younger," I could feel my cheeks burning from embarrassment. "But, no. To be honest I haven't done much traveling."

"And what exactly do you want to do when you have completed all of your schooling?"

I felt the weight of pressure on my chest as my mind tried to come up with an eloquent answer.

"The truth of the matter is, sir, that I am not entirely sure at this point," I nervously crossed and then uncrossed my legs. So much for trying to come off as calm and collected.

"I see," he muttered. "Well, I will certainly try my best to write you an acceptable letter of recommendation."

"Is that all?" I asked nervously. My eyes darted around the room until my gaze finally met his.

"That's all," he nodded.

I exhaled a little too loudly and made my way to the door.

"Oh, and one more thing," he called from behind me. "Think about what you want to do with your life past NYU. Because if there's one thing you will learn from life, merely *wanting* something simply isn't enough."

Twenty-five – Olivia

At the first sign of nice weather, Amalia and I hauled ourselves downtown to walk all the river front in Battery Park. It was a very beautiful area in Manhattan. Mostly a tourist spot, the paved pathway along the river walk always offered a beautiful view. Park benches and a few waterfront restaurants made you forget you were in the city for a little while. It was a pleasant respite.

Much more pleasant if I had a cigarette.

We sat on the outside patio of a restaurant called Merchants River House, and slowly sipped white wine while waiting for our food to arrive.

"I almost forgot," Amalia put down her wine glass and folded her hands on the table. "I got Dr. Greenfield to write me a letter of recommendation."

"That's great! When did this happen?"

"A few weeks ago actually," she took another sip of her wine. "Not worrying about him having to write that letter anymore has made me feel so much lighter. Believe it or not, for a few weeks there I completely forgot about having to plan my future. It was wonderful."

"That sounds like a nice break from reality," I laughed.

Amalia simply smiled and then turned her head towards the water. The wind kicked up a notch and I watched as her hair looped around her head. A moment later, the same thing happened to mine. It felt good to be outside. To feel a temperature higher than forty degrees. She stared out there just long enough to make me wonder what she was thinking.

"While we are on the topic of things happening and us forgetting about them," I said, bracing myself for her reaction, "I ran into Hayden about a month ago."

Amalia's eyes blue eyes focused on me as the color in her cheeks paled.

"Why are you just telling me this now?" she asked in a flat tone. "I haven't heard from him at all and you two have been talking?"

I put up my hands in a gesture of peace. "We only talked the one time. I ran into him on 5th avenue while walking to class."

Amalia seemed to regain her composure. Her shoulders relaxed and her eyes softened.

"Amalia," I broached the topic gently. "Why would you get so upset over the mere mention of Hayden? I mean, you did choose Michael over him." I reached across the table and gave her small hand a squeeze. I didn't want her to feel confronted. I wanted her to think about why she responded the way she did when it came to these men.

She stared into space for a moment before taking a rather large sip of her wine. The waiter materialized, dropping off our food and extra napkins. Another few seconds passed before Amalia finally said something.

Hey eyes reddened and cheeks puffed out, she let out three small words.

"I don't know."

The next week Alex and I went by the hotel we were having our nuptials at for a tasting. The amount of food was overwhelming. Essentially, we got to taste every single thing the chef could offer us. That included a chicken dish, a pork disk, a beef disk, and a fish. Not to mention the endless amounts of wine. There were four wines to choose from. What I didn't notice was the server who kept coming around filling up our glasses. By the time we were finishing up dessert, I felt more than a little ill.

When we got home I realized not only was I totally sauced, but Alex was too. After locking the front door, I took off my coat and scarf but didn't stop there. I caught Alex's eye and began to seductively unbutton my shirt. Only I was trashed and it looked more like a mental patient trying to get out of a strait jacket.

"What are you doing?" he said, a slight slur in his voice.

"What do you *think* I'm doing," I replied with the world's worst wink.

Alex quickly peeled off his coat and gloves and a second later we were kissing. His hands were on my face and I struggled to reach his height. Standing on my toes, I teetered back and forth until Alex picked me up and moved me to the couch. Sitting upright, I reached for Alex's shirt and tried to remove it in one swift tug. However his button-down got caught on his undershirt, causing him to flail back and forth on the couch. I reached to help but one of his arms accidentally hit me in the eye.

"Alex," I mumbled, covering my eye with the palm of my hand. "I think we should give up on this task."

Alex finally got both of his shirts off and held them in the air triumphantly. A wide smile spread across his cheeks until he saw my now-bruised eye.

"What happened?" he slurred.

I took a deep breath before saying, "you're a drunk mess and you hit me in the eye."

"Oh no. I'm sorry!" He scrambled to wrap his arms around me. "Here, come lie down with me."

I moved over on the couch and placed my head on his chest. The room was spinning around me and there was a definite possibility of me getting sick as any moment.

"Baby," I whispered. "I'm feeling really bad. I'm going to try to get some sleep."

I looked at his face and saw that not only were his eyes closed, but he was in a deep sleep.

Twenty-six – Amalia

I stared at my computer screen as I tapped my right hand on the desk. I was fully prepared for this. I had decided that I was going to write Cassandra an email. I had it all mapped out in my head. I would ask, *What made you change so much? Does our friendship mean nothing to you? Honestly, what is the matter with you?*

But now that I willing to write it, I was drawing a blank. Every time I began writing a sentence, I ended up deleting it. Some opening lines sounded too friendly while others were bitter and cold. I also couldn't decide between addressing her as Cassandra or Cassie. The anxiety of reaching out to my once-best friend was overwhelming. Not to mention making me feel ridiculous.

I shook my head and just began typing. I wrote how she hurt me last year by her constant absence. How it had been a year since Olivia's engagement party, when she essentially refused to have a real conversation with me about how our friendship had strained. I wrote about how I saw her at the farmer's market and she ignored me. But most of all, I asked her how she was. Was she completely fine without me in her life? Did she miss me at all?

Before I had a chance to delete it, I hit send.

I covered my face with my hands and gently rubbed my eyes. All I could do now was hope she would write back so I could finally get some answers. The ball was in her court.

I pushed my chair back from my desk and glided to my bed. It was a lazy Sunday and I had no plans. Michael hadn't asked me to hang out and I felt weird about asking him. Which made me wonder if that was normal. Things certainly hadn't been that way with Nicholas. I never had to worry about asking him to get together out of fear I might be bothering him. But then again, Michael was different. He had all of the pressures of graduate school and I think that consumed most of his thoughts and energy. I leaned back on my bed until my head hit the pillow. I knew I was being selfish wanting to see him when he was most likely too engrossed in his work to do anything else, but I was busy too. I was in the same program as him and I had to do work-study on top of it.

So why was I the only one who felt bad about us not seeing each other?

I glanced over at my phone on the night stand and felt my eyebrows furrow. When had I become so paranoid about contacting a guy? Grabbing the phone, I felt a strange sense of nerves wash over me. Ignoring it, I scrolled through my contact list until I landed on Michael's number. In lieu of a text message, I decided to call him. After all, what is so strange about a girl calling her boyfriend?

The phone rang four times before I got his voicemail. Slightly annoyed, I left a message.

"Hey, babe. Hope your day is going well. I just wanted to see what you had planned for today. Maybe we can get together later? Call me back."

As I hung up the phone, I couldn't help but feel irritated. He couldn't even answer my call? And who knows how long it'd be before he called me back. These games were to be expected a couple of years ago when he was still figuring things out with Marge. But not anymore.

I was beginning to feel like this relationship was not normal.

Just as I was about to put the phone down it buzzed in my

hand, causing me to jump. A hopeful smile spread across my face. Maybe Michael wasn't being so distant after all. But as I turned the phone over I saw that it wasn't a message from Michael. It was from Hayden.

Hayden was moving to Florida, and I still wasn't sure on the date. Based upon what he said to Olivia it had to be relatively soon.

The two of us had been keeping our distance from one another since we ended things. It was hard on me. Being with Hayden was like dating a best friend. He was kind, patient, and calm. Not to mention very selfless. I thought about him more than I probably should. And most of the thoughts came to me at times like this when Michael was being emotionally unavailable. Bracing myself, I opened the message application on my phone and tapped on Hayden's name.

It was short and to the point. He asked if we could talk.

In person.

Considering Hayden's request, I walked over to my bedroom window and peeked outside. There wasn't much of a view where I lived. Nothing compared to the panoramic vision of New York City that Olivia and Alex's apartment offered. I looked down at the street and saw a few people walking their dogs. The streets were pretty empty for a weekend but watching even a few people outside made me long to get out of my apartment. A moment later I saw a young couple holding hands, laughing as they made their way down the street. I felt a pang of sadness in my chest as I realized that Michael and I were never that affectionate with one another. In fact, besides sex, we were hardly ever physically near one another. We didn't hug or exchange kisses that didn't turn into something further. We didn't hold hands or even cuddle on the couch during a movie.

I took a step back from the window and paced as I wrote Hayden back.

Hey, sure. Is now good?

A few seconds went by and then my phone buzzed again.

Now is good. Can I come by your apartment?

I scanned my apartment. My bed was unmade and littered with clothes. My coffee table was decorated with unopened envelopes and unwashed dishes. And the general state of my floors was less than optimal. I squashed a roach earlier than day and forgot to clean it up. I shook my head and wrote him back.

Actually, can I come to yours?

Moving from my bedroom to the bathroom I ran a hairbrush through my hair while rummaging in the drawer for some concealer. After a slight primping, I darted to my closet to find clothes to wear, but then remembered most of them were scattered across my bed. And floor. Grabbing my favorite pair of jeans that I got for a steal from Nordstrom Rack, I felt a slight sense of worry.

What if Michael finds out about this?

And then I realized, I never know where Michel is or what he is doing when we aren't together. We might be officially a couple, but he wasn't answering my calls. Would he really even care if I was spending time with Hayden?

We were about to find out.

After pulling a flowy light-pink blouse over my head I took once last glance in the mirror as my phone went off again.

Sure. Come over when you're ready.

I snatched my keys off the coffee table and flung my purse over my shoulder.

I was ready.

A short cab ride later, I arrived at Hayden's apartment. He buzzed the door opened so I could come through the entrance and met me at his front door. It was a warm welcome.

"Amalia!" he grabbed me by the waist and pulled me in for a hug. As soon as his arms wrapped around me, I experienced something that I hadn't felt in a long time. The feeling that someone really wanted me in their life. Not just wanted for sex. Wanted for something more.

I couldn't pinpoint it.

"It's really good to see you," I heard myself say. Feeling myself blush, I lowered my head a few inches and let out a small laugh. I hadn't realized how much I missed him.

He looked exactly the same. Brown hair, green eyes, and a gentle, yet masculine, smile.

"Come in!" He led the way into the apartment I had spent so much time in last year. As soon as I walked through the door a rush of memories came flooding back to me. One that stood out in particular was when he asked me to spend Thanksgiving break with him in his hometown of Gainesville, Florida. I turned him down, saying that I needed to spend some time with my family. But the truth was that I was scared.

Hayden wanted so much more from me then I was able to give at the time. Having just come back from Brazil, losing my apartment and my best friend, Cassandra, and still having to see Michael at school really messed with my head. Sometimes I wondered how it would have been if I had met Hayden before I had come to NYU. If he had been the one I could turn to after Nicholas broke up with me.

I wondered if my life would be different now. Maybe Hayden wouldn't be moving away.

Or maybe I'd be moving with him.

I shook the thought out of my head and met Hayden's gaze. Nervously, I asked for a glass of water. I needed something to do with my hands, which were shaking.

Hayden retrieved a glass of water from the tap. The marble counter top by the sink was shining. I wondered if he had done some cleaning once I said that I was coming over. Leading me to the couch where we once used to cuddle and watch movies from, I felt a small flutter of butterflies in my stomach. I smiled at the memories and slowly lowered myself onto the plush sofa. He followed suit and sat down next to me, except unlike in the past there was enough space between us to fit an extra person.

"So, I hear Olivia's getting married," he said, breaking the awkward silence.

"She is!" I perked up, grateful he'd offered something to talk about. "Over the summer. She's getting married at the hotel in SoHo."

"The Mondrian, right?"

"That's the one," I offered him a wide grin. Another long silence passed and I took a gulp of my water to make it a little less uncomfortable.

Hayden didn't look nervous. Or if he did, he was hiding it very well.

"So," I started, putting down my glass on a carefully placed coaster. "What did you want to talk to me about?"

He lowered his head and sighed. His eyes swept the floor and then back up to me. A sad smile tugged at his lips as he began to answer my question.

"Firstly, I am moving to Gainesville at the end of the month."

"The end of this month?" I asked a little louder than I intended.

"Yeah," he sank back further into the couch. "March 30th is moving day."

"I'm happy for you," I uttered. "For your promotion and for getting out of New York. Which I know you have wanted to do for a while now." I paused and considered my next words carefully. "But if I am being completely honest, I kind of wish you weren't moving."

Hayden furrowed his brows and took a deep breath. For a moment, I could have sworn I saw a look of anger flash across his face. But as soon as I saw it, it disappeared.

"Amalia," he sighed. "Why are you saying this to me?" He looked me straight in the eyes. The intensity of his stare was almost too much to handle. "You know how I feel about you." He lowered his head again.

"I know how you *felt*. But it's been about a year since we stopped dating. I would have guessed you'd have moved on by now."

"Sure. I went on a few dates here and there," he nodded. I felt a knot of jealousy, usually monopolized by Michael's actions.

Why did I care if Hayden went on a few dates?

"But," he continued. "I haven't had real feelings for a girl in a long time."

"How long?" I muttered, fearing I already knew the answer.

He paused for a moment and seemed to consider my question. Then another sad smile claimed his face.

"About a year," he reached for his water and took a large gulp.

He pressed his lips into a straight line, and I could see that even though so much time had passed he still wasn't over me.

I wish Michael felt half as strongly as Hayden did.

"You're with Michael now?" he asked, breaking me out of my daze.

I offered him a nod, not really wanting to get into the whole story. Which was what, exactly?

I was in love with Michael, but he couldn't give me the kind of relationship I wanted. Hayden was in love with me but I couldn't give him the commitment he wanted. And deserved. A twisted, proverbial, love triangle which, from where I stood, looked like everyone was on the losing end of.

"Do you ever even think about me, Amalia?" he muttered.

His question caught me off guard. It was so direct compared to dealing with Michael's cryptic and evasive lexicon. Hayden's candor was pretty refreshing.

"Yes," I answered, being just as direct as he was.

"What do you think that means?"

"Honestly?" I took a beat. "I don't know."

Anxious, I reached for my glass of water on the coffee table, but as soon as I leaned forward Hayden caught my hand. The next thing I knew he was kissing me. The kisses were soft, nothing like how Michael and I kissed. I leaned into Hayden, wrapping my arms around him. After a few more seconds of kissing, Hayden pulled away.

"I'm so sorry," he stood up and looked away from me. "That was completely out of line." He turned to me with a look of worry on his face. "You have a boyfriend."

I did have a boyfriend. But what was worse was the fact that I really didn't want that kiss to end.

"We're having problems," I blurted out. As soon as the words came out of my mouth it felt like a weight had been lifted off my chest.

"What do you mean?" Hayden asked. "I just asked you five minutes ago if you were with Michael."

I tugged nervously at the end of my shirt. "We're dating, but he and I aren't really on the same page with each other."

Hayden blinked at me a few times before shaking his head and letting out a rough throaty laugh.

"So, after all of this," his voice rising a bit. "The two of you are finally together and you're unhappy?" He stood up from the couch and stared straight at me.

I looked at the floor, unsure of what exactly to say.

"It's complicated," I stammered. "I want to be with him, but…"

"But what?" Hayden demanded. His eyes were red and glassy. He ran his hands over his head and pressed his eyes together tightly. I had never seen him this upset before.

I nervously picked at my cuticles. "But I don't feel like he really wants to be with me!" It was the first time I had said those words out loud and I was blown away by their power.

I couldn't quite pinpoint my feelings until just now. But there it was, plain as day.

I didn't feel like Michael wanted to be with me. And I never had.

My words seemed to affect Hayden almost as much as they affected me. His eyes softened as he lowered himself back onto the couch next to me.

"Amalia," he said softly. "What's wrong?"

"Nothing," I shifted my weight while stifling tears from falling out of my eyes. Shaking my head, I took a deep breath.

"Everything." I looked over at Hayden, who currently had his arm over the back of the couch. It felt nice to have someone there for me.

"I'm sorry I raised my voice at you," he uttered in a low voice.

"Honestly," I started. "With the way I have treated you I am surprised you are still talking to me at all." I felt a stream of tears roll down my check. With his thumb, he gently wiped them away.

"You're not so bad," he joked.

I offered a half-smile and a full eye roll.

"I love your eyes," he whispered. "So big and blue"

I caught myself holding my breath and let out a sharp exhale.

"So, what was the other thing you wanted to tell me?" I twisted a stray hair through my fingers.

"Pretty much what we just spoke about, how I still have feeling for you," he had a pained look in his eyes. "And that if things don't work out with Michael, I want you to consider moving down to Florida. After you finish school, of course."

My eyebrows involuntarily raised, "Why would I move to Florida?"

"The town I am moving back to, Gainesville, has a lot of job opportunities. Especially for someone with have an advanced degree in behavioral science. Plus the cost of living is so much less, and we all know how much you hate the cold weather…" his voice trailed off.

"I can't just uproot myself and leave New York. It's my home."

"But Amalia," Hayden cocked his head to the side. "You hate living here."

"What are you talking about," I couldn't help but start laughing. "I don't hate living here. I mean, sure, the Arctic blast that lasts for eight months isn't fun, and the price of everything goes up every year, but I love New York."

Didn't I?

"Maybe I'm wrong," he held up his hands in mock defeat. "But when we were together last year I always felt a sadness within you. I know that you're stressed about school, and about what you want to do when you graduate. I know you feel a bit stuck." He paused for a moment. "But I feel like you could thrive in a town like Gainesville."

I was speechless. Hearing Hayden lay it all out for me like that gave me a clarity I never really had before. Maybe I wasn't only miserable because of Cassandra and because of Michael and my relationship. Maybe it had more to do with constantly being broke. From the desolate feeling of living in a 650-square-foot box. And, quite possibly, it was from knowing that even when I did graduate from NYU, I still wouldn't be making enough money to live in more than a tiny apartment. With my student-loan payments, I would almost definitely be living paycheck to paycheck.

That was my future here in the city. Living in a small apartment, hoping to do well enough at work to make ends meet, and forever having this abnormal relationship with Michael.

I felt my cheeks flush and suddenly felt like I couldn't breathe. I stood up from the couch and immediately felt dizzy.

"Amalia," Hayden put a hand on my shoulder. "Are you alright?"

"Yeah. I'm fine," I mumbled as I made my way to the door. "I have to go home."

"Are you sure?" Hayden asked with slight desperation in his voice. "I'm sorry if I made you feel uncomfortable."

"It's not that. I just have to go," I slid past him and darted toward the door.

"Amalia, come on!" he called after me. But it was too late. I was already gone.

Twenty-seven – Olivia

I stood in front of the floor-length mirror, swooning over the way the white lace draped my shoulders. It was my final fitting before the big day and, fortunately enough, the dress fit perfectly.

"Now just don't gain a single pound between now and July," Amalia said in a joking tone.

"Thanks, I'll try!"

"Perfect," the seamstress said, taking a step back to fully admire her handiwork. "Are you happy with the length?"

I nodded. "I am happy with everything. Thank you for doing such a great job with my gown."

I could tell I was beaming with excitement. The wedding was in less than four months, and the countdown had officially begun. If only in my head.

Still smiling, I took a step off the podium and Amalia immediately reached for the train of my dress. She followed me into the dressing room, holding the back of my dress the whole time.

"She really should have bustled this!" Amalia said and she softly let go of the train.

I scooped up the bottom of my dress and closed the fitting-room door.

"I'll be out in a second," I called out. Last time I needed help getting in and out of my dress, but for some reason this time it felt much more natural. I was careful not to put on any make-up today that might stain the most important garment I would ever wear.

While placing the gown in its garment bag I heard Amalia's voice call out to me.

"So I wrote Cassandra an email a few weeks ago," she said with a shaky voice.

"Has she written back?" I zipped up the bag and opened the door to the fitting room, leaving the dress inside, as instructed. When I stepped out, Amalia was inches away from my face.

"No," Amalia nervously looked around the store. "But that's not all I have to share with you."

I raised an eyebrow and crossed my arms. I felt a smirk hit my lips. "What did you do?"

"Well technically it wasn't *me* who did it," she fiddled anxiously with her long necklace.

"Amalia Hastings, what did you do?" I could feel my smile widening. I took too much pleasure in the stories concerning her unstable life.

"I kissed Hayden," she spat out a little too loudly. As soon as she did, she covered her mouth with both of her hands.

A few of the store staff members whipped their heads around to gape at Amalia.

"You kissed Hayden?" I whispered.

"Well, technically he kissed me," she pursed her lips together and clenched her jaw. It seemed like she was waiting for me to reprimand her.

I let out a long sigh and took her by the arm, leading her out of Wedding Atelier. Sadly, I had to leave the dress behind, even though it was my final fitting. The store agreed to look after it until the day before my wedding, when I would come pick it up. Too many things could destroy it between now and July. For example, a drunk friend coming over in hysterics and spilling red wine on it.

Amalia pushed open the door and a stream of sunlight hit our faces. We were both temporarily taken aback to find out it was actually nice outside. Spring was in the air.

Well, almost.

"Want to grab a cup of coffee and talk?" I offered, holding my hand above my eyes to shield some of the glare.

"Yes, please," she muttered dejectedly.

I linked her arm around mine and led her to the closest coffee shop. As we walked down the street, I noticed she looked more like herself today than she had in a long time. Her curls were left untamed and delicately framing her face. She was wearing her converse sneakers instead of the Tory Birch flats she starting donning when she and Michael started seeing each other more often. She had on minimal make-up, from what I could tell just foundation, a hint of blush, and clear lip-gloss. No brightly colored lip color this afternoon. No overpowering perfume. And to tie it all together, she was wearing a light-pink, long-sleeved shirt with a faux leather jacket over it.

I couldn't help but smile as I realized she might be going back to her old self too.

We made our way into the nearest Starbucks, ordered a couple of skimmed lattes, and sat down by a window.

"I don't know what I'm doing," she uttered. She twirled a curl around her index finger and stared deeply into her cup of coffee.

"What do you want to do?" I asked gently. Part of me wanted to probe her with questions. Find out why she acted this way. Why she couldn't just see what was right there in front of her.

"I don't know," she answered softly. "Hayden texted me about a week ago asking to talk in person and we just sort of ended up kissing. I told him afterwards that I was with Michael. He got angry at first, but ultimately let me off the hook."

I took a sip of my coffee, considering my next words.

"Did Hayden tell you when he's moving?"

"He did," she nodded, still looking down. "March 30th."

"Wow. That's next week," I took a long, soothing sip of my coffee. "Do you think you'll see him again before he moves?"

She finally met my gaze. Her blue eyes were glazed over with dolor, and her lips twitched into a sad smile. She shook her head and I understood from the gesture that she couldn't talk about it anymore. I reached over across the table and gave her small hand a squeeze.

"I'm here for you," I said softly.

"I know," one tear rolled out of her eyes and landed on her cheek. "Thank you, Olivia."

I handed her a napkin and she quickly dabbed her eyes. Not that it really mattered. This was New York City. Someone could come and sit down next to you wearing nothing but their boxers and a pair of construction boots and no one would look twice.

"Change of subject," she declared with faux enthusiasm. "Can you believe we only have two months left of school?"

Now it was my turn to feel stressed out. Graduation was in May and I still hadn't heard back from any of the doctoral programs I had applied to. None of us had.

"It went by fast," I shook my head. "Much faster than I could have imagined."

"Think of how much has changed since we all first met," she mustered up a half-smile. "I thought you were dating our TA!"

"I had no idea anything was going on with you and Michael!" I laughed. "The two of you keep secrets very well."

"I'll take that as a compliment," she chuckled. "My roommates! Christina was fine but Liz was a nightmare."

"Oh! Group study sessions in your old apartment," I smiled at the memory. "Those were good times."

Amalia nodded, holding the coffee cup in both hands. "Remember that douche bag Bryce that Cassandra was dating? He was the worst. But then again, he is how I met Hayden."

"Remember Cassandra?" I raised an eyebrow.

A look of pain swept across Amalia's face and then quickly dissolved.

"I'm sorry," I gently slapped my forehead. "I just shoved my

175

foot in my mouth."

"It's fine," she paused to sip her coffee. "I sent her an email, my last-ditch effort. I love Cassie, but there's nothing more I can do. She has changed so much from the person I grew up with that if I met her now–"

"You probably wouldn't want to be her friend anyway?" I cut her off.

"As much as it pains me to say it, yes, that's how I feel."

Amalia and I exchanged a look. Looking back on these past few years made me really grateful to have her in my life. Even if she was a bit wacky at times, I still considered her to be my best friend.

"Promise me one thing," she said, finishing the last sip of her coffee.

"What's that?" I asked.

"That before finals, we'll have one more group study session. Like we used to. But this time I think it should be in your apartment."

"I think that can be arranged," I laughed. "Now you have to promise me something."

Amalia just nodded, waiting for me to continue.

"Promise me you'll consider talking to Hayden again before he moves to Florida."

She looked around, everywhere but at me. Finally she said, "I'll think about it."

"Alright," I collected our paper coffee cups and tossed them in the trash bin. "That's all I ask."

Twenty-eight – Amalia

"How has everything been going for you, Amalia?"

I sat across from Autumn with my legs crossed and my hands folded. Today was our last day of therapy together. Work-study was coming to an end and after this week I would never have to interact with her or Dr. Greenfield ever again.

A grin tugged my lips as I said, "I'm doing pretty well, actually."

"And what about continuing your education after NYU?" she scribbled something on a yellow legal pad. Probably a drawing of her cat. "Have you heard back from any of the doctoral programs that you applied to?"

I shook my head and shifted my weight on the plush chair. "Just one. Hunter College sent me a rejection letter yesterday." I shrugged and Autumn looked at me like I just told her I was dying.

"You seem very cavalier about this?" She pulled her long red hair into a ponytail and then rested her chin on her palm. "Why aren't you more upset?"

"Because I didn't really want to go there," I said, plain and simple. "And I'm trying not to get worked up about something that I didn't even want in the first place."

"Then why did you apply there?" she countered.

"I applied there when I applied to all of the other schools. I don't exactly have a first choice. NYU has been no picnic, but

Hunter is no better than the New School. If I don't get in there, I'll probably muster up some tears."

"Because that's where you really hope to go?" she probed.

"No," I answered, my eyes fixed on hers. "Because I'll have felt like I wasn't good enough to get in. And that will hurt."

"Interesting," she leaned back in her chair.

"What's so interesting, Autumn?" I asked in a slightly defeated tone.

Just fifteen more minutes and then this is over. Fifteen more minutes and I never have to see her again.

"It's interesting, the way you think about rejection," she answered, not missing a beat. "You wouldn't be upset that you didn't get into a program that you have been working toward. But you'd be hurt by the rejection."

To her credit, I saw where she was coming from. It probably sounded strange to those working so hard around me to get into the best doctoral program. They wanted the best education to become the best researchers, or therapists, or professors. My classmates, my friends, even Autumn – they had dreams of conquering the field of study they had been working so hard to break into. Because when you spend nearly a hundred-thousand dollars on your education, getting an office job simply won't cut it. You vehemently fight your way to the top. And that's really what you're doing. *Fighting.* You're put in an exclusive cohort of people who are already brilliant and hard-working for your Master's degree. But you're told merely one day in that there's really only room for ten of you in any given program past this point.

So the rest of your life fades, it disappears. Not because you want it to, but simply because it can't survive.

"The truth is, Autumn, I don't know what school I want to get into because I am still struggling with what I want to do with my life." I braced myself for the next line of questioning. But the next thing she said to me actually took me by surprise.

"A lot of people feel that way in their mid-twenties," she offered me a smile. "It's becoming more and more common for people your age to question their decisions."

I shook my head. "I feel like my life is always at a proverbial crossroads. And I haven't always made the best choices. But the more I think about it, the more complicated it gets."

I heard a tiny beep go off on Autumn's phone, indicating that our session was over. I felt a sense of relief hit me. I could leave now. I didn't have to talk about this anymore.

"Our session is up," she said in a hushed tone. "So now that I am officially no longer your therapist, there is something I want to be honest with you about."

I raised an eyebrow and looked around the room like this was some sort of trick. "Alright," I uttered. "What's that?"

Autumn put down her pen, her legal pad, and her judgmental looks. She took a deep breath and stared off for a minute. She looked like she was struggling with what she wanted to tell me.

"I felt very similarly to how you do when I was your age. I had two choices. After I finished my Master's degree I got an offer from NYU to finish out the rest of my education here. Four to five more years of classes, training–" She trailed off for a moment before saying, "Isolation."

I kept perfectly quiet and still. Suddenly it was Autumn's emotions that were on display, and I was careful not to make any sudden movements.

"I think that's the worst part," she lightly scratched her forehead. "The loneliness."

She caught my eye and quickly cleared her throat. "What none of my friends knew was that I had gotten another offer. One in Los Angeles to study art."

"Really?" I asked. "You don't seem like the–"

"Artistic type?" she finished my sentence. "No, I wouldn't now. Because that life is gone. Along with a lot of my friends and the close relationship I used to have with my family."

I had no idea what to say, but I slowly began to realize what she was telling me. She was telling me that this wasn't the life she had imagined for herself.

"All of this is to say that I had a choice. And for me," she tapped her chest lightly. "It was the wrong choice. So if you're not completely sure if you want to spend the rest of your life doing this, then you have to allow yourself the chance to find something else. Even if you just take a year off. Maybe travel, maybe work at a coffee shop in the Village, it doesn't matter. Just use your time wisely, because it is *your* time. And you're not going to get these years back. This is the kind of life, Amalia, where you have to eat, sleep, and breathe your career. You have to be married to it. You have to *need* it. Because I learned the hard way that *wanting* it simply wasn't enough."

I stared at her for a moment as our eyes locked on one another's. And in the moment, I felt like this girl, who I hardly knew, knew me better than anyone else in my life.

There was nothing else to say except, "Thank you."

She nodded and stood up to walk me to the door. As she reached for the handle, she wished me good luck and congratulations on my upcoming graduation.

I shuffled out of the room and numbly made my way down the hallway and out the front door. Immediately I was ambushed by the hustle and bustle of Washington Square Park.

I took a look around the area. An elderly couple holding hands and sitting on a bench. A few teenagers standing a little too close to the fountain, threatening to splash one another. A group of undergrads that I recognized practicing their latest skateboarding moves. And then there was me. I didn't fit in anywhere.

Taking a few steps further into the park, I stared up at the giant white arch. It was truly beautiful.

A lot of tourists were taking selfies in front of it and I smiled watching them discover for the first time some of New York's beauty.

"Will you take our picture?" A woman in her early thirties

with a Scottish accent asked me. I smiled and nodded, taking the camera from her hands.

She darted over to who I assumed was her husband and the two of them immediately wrapped their arms around one another.

I held the camera up and positioned the happy couple in the middle, careful to get the entire arch in the background.

"Okay," I said softly, my eyes fixed on them for a few extra seconds.

"Smile."

Twenty-nine – Olivia

"Gather around the coffee table everyone," I said in a hurried tone. "Alex has the flash cards, I have the outlines, and Amalia has the coffee. Michael, did you bring anything?"

The three of us turned to him as he retrieved his laptop from his satchel.

"I have all of the notes I've taken since the beginning of the year," he offered. "And an overwhelming need to get an A on this final."

"Sounds good to me," Alex said while lowering himself onto the floor. He smoothed out his dark wash jeans as he landed on the hardwood.

Alex, Amalia, Michael, and I were all sitting crosslegged around the coffee table in my and Alex's living room. As promised, we were having one final group-study session before the end of school.

"Where should we start?" Amalia asked, inching a bit closer to Michael. He didn't seem to notice.

"Why don't we start with our most recent notes and work our way backwards?" Michael answered without looking at her.

We all nodded, flipping through notebooks and textbooks.

I looked over at Amalia, doing a quick body scan of her outfit. Just like the other day, she was dressing more like her old self. Although her hair was flat-ironed, her outfit consisted of black jeans, a grey longsleeved shirt with a picture of a band on it that

I had never heard of, and her trademark Converse sneakers.

A part of me wanted to ask her if the way she was dressing had anything to do with her realizing that Michael probably wasn't the right guy for her, but I thought it best not to put the idea in her head. She was stubborn, and there was a possibility she'd stay with him just to prove she could. Even if deep down it wasn't what she really wanted. She flipped over a flash card and let out a sigh. This final was going to drive all of us crazy.

After a few minutes of studying, Michael chimed in and asked Alex and I how we were feeling about our upcoming nuptials.

"Excited," Alex grinned. "I can't wait."

I smiled and reached for his hand under the coffee table. "I feel the same way."

Amalia and I exchanged a glance, quickly followed by her turning her gaze to Michael. I watched as she reached for Michael's hand under the table. He didn't pull away, but he didn't acknowledge it either. She looked right at him and for a moment I could feel her pain.

I cleared my throat and then clandestinely slid my phone off of the table and sent Amalia a text asking her if she talked to Hayden yet.

Her phone vibrated loudly against the wood and she flinched at the sound. Michael and Alex looked up from their computers and for a second I could have sworn I saw Michael roll his eyes.

"You should get that," I said without looking up. "It could be important."

Amalia grabbed her phone and I watched her eyes scan the message. Her face paled as she dropped her cell into her lap. She met my eyes and slowly shook her head no. I smirked at her reaction and clapped my hands together to get everyone's attention.

"Hey, you guys. Follow me," I stood up and walked over to the kitchen area. Standing on my tip-toes, I grabbed four glass champagne flutes from the cabinet.

"What's all this?" Amalia asked?

Alex opened the refrigerator and pulled out a bottle of some very expensive champagne. "Olivia and I have been saving this for a special occasion," he said. "And what could be more special than the four of us taking our last final exam and then finishing out our time at NYU together?"

Michael turned to Amalia and gave her a small kiss on her forehead. She smiled in delight, and wrapped her tiny arms around his waist.

"I couldn't agree more," Michael said. "Graduation is right around the corner."

"Would you do the honors?" Alex handed the bottle to Michael and a moment later the cork popped off loudly and champagne started to spill.

"Easy there!" I laughed, trying to catch the bubbly with my glass. Michael handed me the bottle and I starting pouring everyone a glass.

For a moment, the four of us just looked at one another. I felt a rush of memories come flooding back to me. Meeting Amalia for the first time and not being sure if we were going to get on well. Alex approaching me after class one day and asking me to get lunch with him. It felt like yesterday and now he and I were getting married! I could tell Amalia was feeling nostalgic too. Her cheeks were turning red and her eyes watered, threatening to spill over. She lifted her glass up a little higher and I followed suit.

"To graduation," Alex declared.

"To graduation!" we all repeated in unison.

Thirty – Amalia

It was the night before Hayden was moving out of Manhattan to his former hometown of Gainesville, Florida, and I was sitting on a bench in Zuccotti Park reading the latest Sara Shepard book. Zuccotti Park was particularly beautiful at night, or in the very early morning hours. During the day, it was a small gathering place for business types who worked on Wall Street to sit and have their lunch outside. It was also the home for the infamous Occupy Wall Street protests. But right now, at eight o'clock at night, it was downright peaceful. Encircled by trees, the small park had a secluded feeling to it even though it was smack in the middle of the financial district in downtown Manhattan. The sunken seating area was illuminated by glowing lights any time of year, giving the park a fairy-tale feeling.

Ever since I had accompanied my father into the city as a young child this area had always held a special place in my heart. My dad and I would take the bus into Manhattan from Staten Island, the borough I grew up in. After standing in the grueling cold, waiting for the bus in the early hours of the morning, my dad and I would enter Manhattan through the Holland Tunnel and within minutes I was greeted by the awe-inspiring view of downtown New York City.

I smiled as I remembered telling Hayden that story just last year.

A couple of hours earlier I had reached out to Hayden, asking him if he would come downtown to meet me here. One last face-to-face before he left for good. Just as I finished the chapter I was reading I heard footsteps coming from behind me. I lowered the book onto my lap and looked up to find Hayden standing above me. He was wearing casual jeans and a t-shirt with a black leather jacket over it all.

"Hi," I breathed.

He smiled and held my gaze. Barely audibly he said, "Hey."

I pulled my dark-blue cardigan a little tighter around my shoulders. Not necessarily because I was cold, more because I was nervous. Hayden took a seat next to me on an illuminated bench. We were the only ones in the park at this time of night. It was completely peaceful.

I tried to remember the last time I had felt peace. It had been a while.

"Can you believe it's almost April?" I uttered in a near-whisper.

"Graduation is right around the corner for you," he said. I nodded offering up a sad smile.

"What's wrong?" he asked, gently placing a supportive hand on my knee. Even through my jeans I could feel the warmth of his skin. I felt a tiny buzzing feeling followed by the faintest hint of longing after he moved his hand off of me.

"Nothing," I shrugged. "At least nothing should be wrong."

Hayden cocked his head to the side and let out a soft chuckle. "You're a very complicated girl, Amalia."

"Tell me about it," I muttered, tucking a curl behind my ear. I sheepishly raised my eyes back up to his. A fresh wave of nerves hit me.

"So," he said, looking down at his feet. "What are your plans for next fall?"

"Well, if you had asked me that question yesterday I would have said I had no idea. But I actually got my acceptance letter into Hunter College today," I declared through a fake grin.

Hayden perked up. "Congratulations! Was that your first choice?"

"Thank you. And, no," I shook my head. "Columbia was. But honestly, it was a long shot. Plus it's incredibly expensive. So is the New School. But now I don't have to worry about any of that. It looks like I'll be going to Hunter for their Ph.D. program. Which is much cheaper.

Hayden paused for a moment. Without a sound he just looked deep into my eyes. I had always felt a connection to him, but for some reason now it felt stronger than ever. Even after everything we had been through. Even when I knew he was moving four thousand miles away the next day. A part of me wished I could spend the rest of the night staring into those eyes.

"I really wish you weren't moving," I heard myself say.

Hayden looked off toward the now-empty streets of Broadway. "Amalia, that's not fair."

"I know it's not," I uttered. Before I realized what was happening, tears starting to fall down my cheeks. They were hard and fast, not like a stream. More like a hailstorm.

Hayden shifted his weight and faced me. "Please don't cry."

"I don't even know why I am!" I said, a little louder than I intended to. "I should be happy. I got into a Ph.D. program. I got–"

"Michael?" he cut me off before I could finish.

"I guess," I replied. "So why aren't I happy?" The sounds of the city seemed to stop for a moment and all I could hear was my and Hayden's breathing.

"Amalia, have you ever asked yourself what you want?" Hayden asked me, with a look of near-pity in his eyes. "I mean, not for right this moment, but in general. What you want out of life?"

"Not really," I admitted, nervously pulling on the hem of my cardigan. "I have spent so many years just chasing what I thought I should want. I chased Nicholas when our relationship was breaking down. Then I spent the next few years chasing Michael and the idea of finally getting my happy ending with him. Now I'm chasing

187

down more student loans and five more years of school before I even start my career. And, to be perfectly honest, I have no idea what that's going to be."

"I can see you teaching," Hayden cut in.

"Really?" I let out a soft chuckle. "You mean at a university?"

"That's exactly what I mean," he smiled. "You know, there are a few universities around Gainesville," I gave him a playful nudge and he laughed.

I took a beat, thinking about what Hayden said about me knowing what I wanted. Clearly I didn't.

"I think I'm going to head home," he said, breaking my train of thought. He and I stood up at the same time and pulled each other in for one final hug.

"Thank you, Amalia," he said through what sounded like tears.

"For what?" I whispered.

"For showing me what I want out of life," he stated. "I always knew that things like money and power weren't even going to bring me happiness and when I met you it validated all of that. I love you, Amalia. I know you don't feel that way about me back, but it has never gone away for me. You have shown me what happiness really is, and the meaning of a full life. What is and what's isn't worth chasing. And for that, I will always love you."

I just stared at him, feeling my heart tug in my chest. I felt so confused. Why couldn't Michael feel this way about me?

"And the offer stands," he continued. "If you get tired of old New York, then you are more than welcome to move down to Gainesville and try out a new kind of life. I'd be there for you every step of the way."

Before I could say anything, Hayden turned on his heel and quickly walked down the street. I stood there, in the middle of the park, trying to catch my breath.

I couldn't tell you why, but at the moment something snapped in me.

Things would never feel the same.

Thirty-one – Olivia

"I can't believe how unflattering these commencement gowns are!" I held mine up in its plastic wrapping. Even condensed into square of purple and blue polyester, I could picture how ridiculous we would all look in these gowns.

"We'll only be in them for a few hours," Alex said as an undergrad with a name tag handed him his cap and gown.

I looked around the long hallway. I saw a few people I knew picking up their graduation gear further down. There was August, Dr. Greenfield's favorite student, talking with a girl who looked familiar. I realized it was Angela. She brushed August's arm as she giggled at something he said. I furrowed my brow. There was no way he was saying anything funny.

"I think we've got everything we need here," Alex said, scanning our materials. "Ready to take final exams?"

I spun my head around, having forgotten for a few minutes that final exams were today. The last tests we'd be taking in the Master's program. I pursed my lips together and shook my head.

"I'm ready to get them over with," I looped my arm around Alex and we headed toward the elevator. As I took a step forward to hit the down button, someone jumped in front of me and I took a step back.

"Hey, guys!" Angela greeted us with a big wave and an even

bigger smile. "Did you hear I got the Ph.D. program at Sarah Lawrence?"

"Wow that's great news!" Alex responded. I knew he was putting on a good face. Just this morning I had gotten acceptance letters to both Columbia and NYU, but nothing had come yet for Alex. I knew he would get into one of those schools. He was the Valedictorian for goodness sake!

"What about you two?" Angela pushed on. "Where will you be next fall?"

"Well, no matter where we end up, we'll be together," I declared. "But our first choice is to stay here at NYU."

"I hope that works out for the both of you," she uttered. Her concentration seemed to be breaking down as she scanned the hallways. "Do you by any chance know where Michael got into school?"

I felt both of my eyebrows shoot up and my teeth bite my lip. This girl would not give it up!

"I'm not sure," Alex said. "I haven't gotten a chance to talk to him about it yet."

"Are him and Amalia still dating?" she asked quickly.

"Yup," Alex and I answered in unison.

"Oh," her face dropped and her heavily glossed lips twisted into a pout. Alex and I exchanged a glance as he slowly shook his head. I had to bite my tongue to keep from laughing.

"We should really get downstairs," I reached passed her and pushed the elevator button. "We don't want to be late for our final exams."

"No, of course not!" she tossed her long brown hair from side to side. "One more thing. I'm having a graduation party at my apartment. You should all come!"

"We'll have to let you know," I replied. "We still have a lot of wedding planning to do."

"Oh, come on!" she insisted. "It will be fun, I promise."

As if on cue, the elevator arrived. Alex and I stepped inside but Angela hung back.

"Are you coming?" I asked, mildly irritated from her perkiness.

"I'll meet you down there," she answered. "I just want to make sure I tell August about my party."

I nodded and pushed the elevator button to let us out at the bottom floor. "See you later."

The door closed just as Alex's phone made a chirping noise from his pocket. He let out an exasperated sigh and shoved the phone back into his jacket pocket.

"What is it?" I leaned over to sneak a peek at his phone.

"Just got a text from Michael," he shook his head. "Looks like we're all going to Angela's party."

Thirty-two – Amalia

I re-read the email over and over again. It was short, only three sentences.

AMALIA,

I wrote a letter of recommendation on your behalf for all of the schools you applied to. Sorry I haven't been able to tell you sooner. I hope you have received some good news from the schools you've applied to.
Regards,
Dr. Greenfield.

Graduation was this morning. I had to be at Yankee Stadium up in the Bronx two hours from now. I knew it would be cutting it close but the letter made me feel like I had to go see Dr. Greenfield and thank him in person for writing those letters for me. His support was most likely the main reason I got into Hunter College, who were already pressuring me for a deposit for next fall.

They wanted a commitment.

I was already dressed. I had on a light-pink dress and the more comfortable pair of black flats I owned. I had on a bit more make-up that usual in case my parents wanted to take tons of pictures. Which they probably would. Aaron couldn't make it down to the graduation – he was still taking final exams. I was bummed he couldn't be there, more than anything I just wanted the day to be over with.

I wasn't big on pomp and circumstance.

Pulling my hair to one side of my shoulders I swiped on a coat of red lip-gloss, hoping to give my face some color against these hideous purplish gowns. Taking a deep breath, I gave myself one more look in the mirror.

"Okay, NYU," I said aloud. "One last hurray."

Slowly making my way to the door I grabbed my cap and gown, flinging the gown over my shoulder. I reached for my purse and keys and felt a wave of sadness. A part of me had wished Hayden would have offered me congratulations today, but I hadn't heard anything from him yet. It had been six weeks since he moved, and we had only exchanged two emails. I really missed him.

Another person who still hadn't written back was Cassandra. How many months had it been since I contacted her? Three?

I let out an exasperated sigh, shaking my head. I gave up hope a long time ago that she would contact me on graduation, but the disappointment was still there.

I walked quickly out of my apartment and hailed a cab to NYU to see if I could quickly see Dr. Greenfield before he left for the day. When I got to his office the door was opened and he was sitting at his desk, covered over with paperwork.

"Is this a good time?" I asked quietly.

Dr. Greenfield looked up from his desk. "Um, yes." He pushed some papers into his drawer. "Please have a seat, Amalia."

"That's okay," I said as politely as possible. "I just wanted to stop by before graduation to thank you for the letters you wrote on my behalf. Because of you I got into Hunter College."

He pursed his lips together and gave me a nod. "You're thinking of accepting their offer? Five more years of school to obtain your Ph.D.?"

I looked around the room, suddenly feeling uncomfortable. "Well, yeah. Wasn't that the point of all of this?"

"The point of what, exactly?" he stood up and walked around to the front of his desk. "Of life?"

"I'm not sure I understand," I shook my head. "I thought this is what you wanted for me? For me to buckle down and get into a good program to continue my education."

He rubbed his eyes and for the first time ever, smiled at me. It was quick and it was small, but it was a smile. I was sure of it.

"What I wanted for you, was to figure out what you wanted out of life." He smoothed out his tweed tie.

"Okay, well here you go," I held up my cap and gown for emphasis. "I am graduating in an hour, I got into a Ph.D. program here in New York, I have an apartment, and I have a boyfriend. Hell, I have it all!"

"But is that really what you want?" he pressed on in a calm voice. "Do you want to stay in New York City for the rest of your life? Because if you continue to go to school here, you will. I have seen it time and time again. My students, who have never traveled, stay here because it's what they know. It's what they think is comfortable."

"I don't understand why you're trying to talk me out of this?" I answered defensively. "Why does everyone keep telling me to leave New York?"

"Because you're not happy here, Amalia," he spat out. "Because you think you have to do this. You have to keep going to school, get a job in this field, stay with your boyfriend and hope that everything I just mentioned works out. But let me ask you honestly, is there nothing else in life that you want? No one else? Do you want to get married? Have a family? Or can you honestly say that you are prepared and willing to dedicate your life to your job, because that is what you will be doing. And some of my students should do that. I push them to do that."

"But not me," I whispered. "Because you don't think I'm good enough."

"No," he said quickly. "It's actually because you remind me a lot of myself when I was your age. And in your position."

"What do you mean?" I asked in a near-whisper.

"I was going to school in Chapel Hill, North Carolina, when I met a girl. We were in the same graduate program together. Halfway through our time at school, we started dating and fell deeply in love. We were together for three years when the opportunity came for me to teach in another town, Charlotte. She still had a year left in the program and the truth was I could have stayed in town. I was offered teaching jobs at two other universities in the area, but I let my overwhelming passion for success and money trump my relationship."

I was shocked by Dr. Greenfield's confession. Then it suddenly hit me. The picture in his office, the reason he was always shoving things into his desk. His miserable demeanor. He couldn't stop thinking about his ex-girlfriend, even all of these years later.

"Did you ever try to get her back?" I asked gently.

"I did," he nodded. "But I waited too long. I always thought I'd get over her, meet someone else and get married when the time was right. But two years passed and I was still as in love with her as I always had been. I went to visit her one day, getting her address from a mutual friend. I showed up at her door ready to apologize. Ready to offer to quit my job and move back. Or convince her to move and come live with me in Charlotte. When I finally got to speak to her, she didn't want to hear it. She was so hurt by what I had done to her that she said she could never feel the way she felt for me again."

He looked up at the ceiling and pressed his lips into a line. "It's been decades, and I can honestly say that was the most painful moment of my life."

I didn't know what to say. I touched my face to make sure I wasn't gaping at him. This man, who I had hated for the past two years was going through pain and regret and if I wasn't careful, that could be me when I got older.

"I'm so sorry," I offered.

"Amalia," he muttered my name as usual, never to be said with full strength. But something was different this time. He wasn't using the familiar, judgmental tone I had become accustomed to.

"At the end of it all, it's just you you're left with," he continued. "Some people say life is short, and there's no denying that." He glanced down at the picture on his desk for a moment, taking a deep breath in the process. "But life is also *long*." He looked up from the photo, and his eyebrows popped up like two arrows on his forehead. "*Too* long to choose a path that will lead you nowhere. Much too long not to follow your heart."

As he took a step closer to me, I could feel tears forming in the back of my eyes. But it didn't matter. I was stronger now. But still not strong enough to know what to say.

"I wish I had known sooner," he muttered in a near-whisper. "But you still have time. You have a *choice*."

Didn't I always? But when had I chosen wisely? I thought about Hayden's offer to join him in Gainesville. I could feel the side of my lip pulling my face into a grimace. Dr. Greenfield didn't seem to notice.

"Don't choose poorly," he shook his head. If I looked close enough, I could see the sparkle of tears beginning to form in his brown eyes. "And congratulations on your commencement and acceptance into Hunter College. You worked hard and you deserve it."

I turned my head away and reached for the door, but it was no use. His words had already penetrated something deep inside me. Perhaps it was something I had known all along.

I could almost hear Autumn's voice gloating in my head.

In psychology this is referred to as a "breakthrough".

I scrambled through a crowd of families and security to finally make my way to the gathering area. I spotted Michael chatting with Olivia and darted toward them.

"Hey!" I panted. "Can you help me put this stuff on?" I was talking to both of them, but it was Olivia who helped me out.

"Where were you?" she asked, taking the cap and firmly placing it on my head. "You may need some bobby pins, hang on."

Michael rubbed my back, trying to help me calm down. I looked up at him and smiled and he offered me a quick kiss.

"Happy graduation day," I whispered to him.

"Same to you, babe," he muttered with a grin.

I looked over at Olivia, who had one bobby pin in her hand and another in her mouth. I bent down so she could fasten this horrible excuse for a hat to my straight hair. I figured if I left it curly, the hat wouldn't have fit.

"So, where were you?" she mumbled through the bobby pins.

"Oh, I was with Dr. Greenfield. I wanted to thank him for his letter of recommendation and let him know I got into Hunter College."

"Awesome!" Michael said with genuine enthusiasm.

Olivia finished her handiwork and immediately pulled me in for a hug. "That's great news!"

"Yeah," I mustered. "I'm glad I got accepted." It wasn't technically a lie, I *was* glad I got accepted. But after Dr. Greenfield's speech, I had no idea what I was going to do.

"What about you, Michael?" Olivia asked. "Where have you heard back from?"

I looked down at the ground and steadied myself. This was the part of my and Michael's story where he would tell me he didn't know where he was going to go. He had applied to Ph.D. programs both here in New York and also others out of state.

"Well," he started, biting his lower lip. "I got into The New School, Columbia University, and Pepperdine University."

"Pepperdine?" Olivia said in a shocked tone. "As in California?"

"It's a big decision," Michael nodded, his tassel bobbing back and forth. It would be funny if it wasn't such a tragic moment.

"That's definitely a big move to consider," I uttered. "California is over three thousand miles away."

I'm sure he already knew that, but I just felt I had to add that in for emphasis. If he moved away, there was no way our relationship could survive. We lived ten miles away from each other now and we were hanging on by a thread.

"What about Alex?" Michael transitioned. He certainly was good at avoiding things he didn't want to talk about.

Olivia's eye widened at the sound of her fiancé's name. I thought of how wonderful it must be to feel that way. Just happy and easy. Not hearing someone's name and sorting through all of the problems you're having. To be able to talk about them and tell whoever's asking that everything's just fine. To just be, you know, normal.

"What about you and Alex?" I asked, not commenting further on Michael's inevitable departure to California.

"Well, I was waiting a while to hear back, but we both got into the program here at NYU!" she did a little victory jump. "So we'll be staying right here."

"Speaking of Alex," Michael chimed in. "Where is he?"

The rest of the people in our program were lining up in alphabetical order and getting ready to walk into the stadium.

"He's going to be sitting up on the stage so he's not coming in with the rest of us," she smiled proudly.

"That's right," Michael nodded. "He's our valedictorian."

I could sense a small amount of resentment in his voice and for some reason it made me smirk. Luckily, Michael hardly ever looked at me so it went unnoticed.

"We should line up," I said, pointing to the growing line of students. "We don't want to miss our chance to walk across the stage and be handed a blank piece of paper."

"I'll see you two later at the party!" Olivia waved and quickly headed to find her place in line.

I had to think about what she meant, but then I remember the party at Angela's apartment tonight.

The last place on earth I wanted to be.

I turned to face Michael. For a moment it seemed like it was just the two of us. The noise of the outside world had disappeared as the last few remaining students made their way inside.

"Are you nervous?" he asked. His dark eyes were fixed on mine, but it felt different. I didn't feel the usually consuming passion I did when I looked at him today. It just felt like I was looking at someone I knew.

Or more accurately, someone I didn't.

"I am a little nervous, yeah."

"I hate these things," he rolled his eyes and reached for my hands. "All of the staring and the picture taking."

"And the hugging and the questions," I replied.

"So, Amalia Hastings, where do you see yourself in five years?" Michael smiled at me warmly.

I wanted so badly to say, "With you." But I knew it would scare him. Even worse, the thought was beginning to scare me.

"I see myself being able to answer that question the next time someone asks it."

Michael put his arms around me and pulled me in for a hug. I let my head rest against his chest, listening to the sound of his heart beating. Letting out a deep sigh I took his hands in mine and pulled away from his embrace.

"We should really get inside," I muttered. As soon as the words left my mouth, I felt my phone buzz in my pocket.

"After you," he gestured toward the wide open doors.

I made my way to the long line of students and stood with the ones next to the sign marked H. Michael made his way to the R's. The line started to move up as I pulled my phone out of my pocket. My heart sank when I saw it was a text from Hayden. It was short and to the point.

Happy graduation, Amalia. I hope you get everything you're looking for.

I smiled and then grimaced, realizing it reminded me of the letter Christina had left for me when she moved out of the apartment. Did everyone see me as this lost cause who needed to straighten their life out?

More importantly, were they right?

Thirty-three – Olivia

I sat through three painfully boring speeches until Alex finally took the podium to address the graduating class as their valedictorian. He looked nervous, more nervous than when he asked me to marry him, actually. My eyes were fixed on him and I willed him to look in my direction so I could give him a reassuring smile. But there was no way he'd ever be able to make me out in this crowd.

From what I could see, at the distance I was at, he kept his hands behind his back as he took a step closer to the microphone.

"Welcome, my fellow graduates," he started. The students started cheering and the faculty applauded in their reserved way. Out of the corner of my eye I spotted Dr. Greenfield. He too was applauding, but was surprisingly putting a little more effort into it than the rest of his colleagues.

"Orientation day, three years ago, I sat in an auditorium-sized classroom and didn't know a single person. I looked to my left, I looked to my right, and I realized one of these people would not make it through this program. They would crack under the pressure, or have to surrender their time to more pressing matters, such as financial or familial needs. And throughout my journey here at NYU, we have lost a few fellow classmates for such reasons. But as I look around here today I can say without hesitation that most of you made it."

A roar of cheers and applause vibrated through Yankee Stadium as if Alex Rodriguez had just hit a home run.

Alex let out a laugh and placed his hands on the top of the podium. "And don't think there haven't been times when I have felt like this was all too much for me. But that's the thing about this program. If you don't eat, sleep, and breathe school then you won't make it. Having said that, that doesn't make us any better than them, or them any less than us. And I can't say I definitely would have gotten through all of it without the support of my wonderful fiancé, Olivia Davis."

I felt my face turn red and I buried it in my hands, nearly knocking off my cap.

"And she's probably really embarrassed that I said that, but I had to mention it!" he chuckled, no longer nervous about the hundreds of people staring at him.

"I feel so privileged to have gotten to spend my time learning from some of the toughest and brightest professors I have ever met. Meeting the best friends I ever had, and falling in and out of love with New York more times than I can count."

I saw a lot of people nod along when Alex said that.

Standing up a little taller, Alex raised his right hand and gently took hold of the gold tassel hanging from his cap.

With the tassel in his hand he declared, "So now I'd like to take this opportunity to congratulate you all. To everything we've been through, and to everything that will come. To the next chapter in our journey, and to the class of 2015!"

Synchronously we all moved our tassels from the right side of our caps over to the left and shouted, "To the class of 2015!"

Thirty-four – Amalia

Angela's apartment was packed with students I had never even seen before. It was only a one-bedroom and people were practically spilling into the hallway. The four of us were standing in a corner, not socializing, and sipping warm beer out of plastic cups. Angela herself was sitting on her couch and making out with August Marek. Olivia and I looked at each other and cringed.

"One hour," Olivia declared to Alex. "We're only staying here one hour."

"That won't be a problem," Alex patted her on the back and then took another sip of beer.

I looked around the crowded room and then caught Michael's eye. He gave me a wink. We were all in a good mood. We survived graduation, which included all of our parents taking endless pictures of us, including one of the four of us standing in front of the arch in Washington Square Park. Michael's parents weren't around for the photo session, they just met him for dinner when we were all finished.

I had now known Michael for three years and still hadn't met his parents. The worst part was, I was completely used to it. If his parents, whose names I couldn't even remember right now, had shown up for pictures in the park I would have died of shock.

"Hey," I said to him, placing my plastic cup on a nearby shelf.

"Can we talk?"

Olivia and Alex weren't really paying attention to us so I figured it was a good time to sneak off. Angela's apartment had a small balcony that overlooked pretty much nothing. Her apartment was on the lower east side, no great views, but I wasn't stepping outside for the sights.

I was stepping outside to have a serious talk with my boyfriend.

Michael followed me out and gently shut the sliding glass door behind us. The noise suddenly lessened and I could hear myself think again.

"What's going on?" he asked, reaching for both of my hands. His touch sent a warm buzz through me. Leave it to Michael to find a way to weaken me when I wanted to be strong.

"We need to talk about this fall," I spat out.

"Right now?" He asked, his eyes narrowing.

"I can't keep these feelings to myself anymore," I said quietly. "Michael, we have been dating on and off for years now. We are finally together, finally in a real relationship, and I feel like I am the only one doing any of the work."

"What are you talking about?" he asked, his voice turning edgier.

"I'm talking about the possibility of you moving to the other side of the country and not even talking to me about it. I'm talking about you constantly breaking plans with me and never even thinking about how it would make me feel. I get it, you were busy this semester – we all were. But it's like our relationship and our future means nothing to you. And I know you're not a "take it as it comes" kind of guy. You're a planner. You're smart, and competitive, and calculating. You didn't apply to Pepperdine on a whim, you applied there because there's a part of you that wants to move away. And it's the same part of you that ignored the fact that you're in a relationship and completely neglects me."

There, I had said it. For a second I regretted it all. I couldn't believe everything I had just said. But there was no going back from this. He had to know how I felt. I couldn't carry this anxiety around with me any longer.

"Amalia," he spoke calmly but angrily. "I don't think I should have to consult you in every decision I make."

"Get real, Michael," Now it was my turn to be angry. "This isn't about every decision. This is about you not factoring our relationship into your life."

"What do you want from me?" he was nearly shouting now. He threw his hands in the air and spun around. He made a fist to punch the wall, but then unclenched his hand and dropped it to his side.

"I want a normal fucken life!" I shouted. "I want to make plans with someone and not *expect* them to not show up. I want a boyfriend who reaches for the phone and calls me every once in a while. And I'm sorry, but it definitely isn't normal to consider moving to California without so much as a conversation."

He reached for me but I pulled away before he could touch me.

"Don't," I shook my head. "I'm so done with this. It took all of these years to get you to just be exclusive with me. I'm not going to spend any more of my time convincing you to be with me. It's pathetic. And anyone who makes me feel this pathetic doesn't deserve my love."

For a moment we stared at each other. I knew he wouldn't say anything back. I knew he wouldn't tell me I was wrong, or try to change my mind. We were completely done.

Hell, we were done months ago.

I opened the sliding door, darted through the party and walked out of the door.

Finally, I felt truly free.

Thirty-five – Olivia

"Open your eyes for me," the make-up artist asked. "I want to get this eye-liner perfect."

"You look beautiful," Amalia said to me. Her hair and make-up had been done first and now she was sitting on the bed in the hotel room in a satin robe that read "maid of honor". I didn't have a lot of friends from home that I was still close to, so when it came time to pick bridesmaids I asked my two cousins, Jen and Lindsey. They had already finished getting ready and were with my parents, keeping the photographer occupied.

"You're all done, sweetheart," the make-up artist tapped me on the shoulder.

She packed up her oversized case and headed out the door. Just as my mother entered the room. She was wearing a capped-sleeve, gold-toned gown with black, Christian Louboutin pumps. Her brown hair hung straight to her shoulders and she wore minimal jewelry, just pearl studs.

"You look beautiful, Mom," I stood up to give her a hug.

"Thank you, sweetheart," she gently hugged me back, afraid to smudge anything. "Hello, Amalia."

Amalia popped her head out and waved. "I'm actually going to put on my dress now. I'll give the two of you a moment."

"Your father is outside waiting to come in," my mom said softly.

She studied my face and then gave me a look of something I had never seen from her before. A look of approval.

"Can I put on my gown first?" I asked in an excited tone. "The photographer will be in here in ten minutes and this way she can get some family shots in."

"Of course," my mom walked over to my gown, which was hanging on the closet door. She gingerly took the straps off of the hanger and asked, "May I?"

I smiled and nodded.

A full ten minutes later, my gown was on, buttoned, and bustled. Amalia called from the bathroom, "Can I come out now?" and I told her to get her butt out here.

She stepped out of the bathroom in her pitch-black, floor-length gown. The color might have been inappropriate for a summer wedding, but by the time the ceremony began it would be after six o'clock, and the invitation had said black tie. She looked gorgeous, but I could tell she was nervous. It had been decided before their break-up that Michael would be ushering her down the aisle, and neither one of them wanted to inconvenience us by having us rearrange the groomsmen.

"You look absolutely stunning," she said in a small voice.

"Thank you," I whispered. Tears started to form in my eyes and I immediately blinked them back. The absolute last thing I needed was to stain this dress with black mascara tears.

"Don't you dare cry!" she laughed, handing me a tissue from the night stand.

"Knock, knock," the photographer, Allie, stuck her head through the front door of my hotel room. "Is everybody decent?"

"Yes," my mother answered. A beat later Allie and my father were standing in front of me. My dad looked as if he was going to burst into tears at the look of me in my dress.

"Can I get a few shots of the three of you? And then some of you and your best friend?" Allie asked.

"My maid of honor," I corrected her teasingly. "But also my

best friend."

Amalia sat back down on the bed and waited patiently for my family and I to get our portraits out of the way.

My parents stood on either side of me as the photographer said, "A little closer together now. Okay, smile!"

Thirty-six – Amalia

I saw my phone light up on the night stand just as Olivia and I finished up taking some pictures together. Mostly posed and serious but a few funny. I suggested going outside and having her run around SoHo in her wedding dress, but she shot me a look and I dropped the subject.

"Olivia," the photographer called to her as she was heading out the door. "Kim, the hotel's wedding coordinator, is going to be up here in ten minutes to bring you down for the ceremony."

"Which means I should go now," I turned to Olivia. She widened her eyes and pushed out a long breath. Her parents would be staying with her until the last minute so I knew she'd be alright.

"I'm nervous," she whispered. "What if I fall?"

I looked down at her feet. She had on lavender-colored flats.

I cocked my head to the side and said, "You'll be fine."

Reaching for my phone and my bouquet, I looked her in the eye and said, "Goodbye, Olivia Davis."

She smiled, knowing exactly what I meant.

My heels clacked on the marble floor as I glanced down at my phone and saw I had a new email alert. I pulled myself over to the wall and leaned against it as I scrolled through my emails.

There it was, a message from Cassandra. Of course, the worst possible moment.

I opened the message and slowly read it.

Amalia,

I'm sorry it has taken me so long to get back to you, work has been absolutely swamped. If memory serves, today is Olivia's wedding day. Please offer her my best wishes.

Amalia, I don't really know what to say in terms of our friendship. Honestly, I just have to focus on my career right now and don't have the time to commit to the type of friendship you want. I don't even have time to date.

The truth is, I do miss having you in my life. I miss our Sunday brunches and late-night phone calls. But that all seems so impossible for me now. I am up for another promotion and I know if we made plans, there's a probability I'd end up breaking them.

I do wish the best for you, and hope you're happy.
Cassie

I read it again, just to make sure I didn't miss anything. It was incredible, she didn't think she did anything wrong. I felt my blood pressure rise and anger burrow its way outward in my chest. But then I felt something else.

Nothing.

It was the way I felt about Nicholas, and how I had begun to feel about Michael. I had reached my tipping point with all of them. Pouring myself into these toxic relationships time and time again, only to get hurt. And foolishly, keep coming back for more.

I let out a sound that sounded somewhere between a snort and a sigh and put my phone back into my black sparkly clutch. I was so done with people who were done with me.

"Hey," a voice from behind me muttered.

I turned around to see Michael in a tuxedo. There was no denying he looked great, but it wasn't making my stomach flip the way it usually would.

"Hey," I smoothed out my gown.

"You look beautiful," he said with a sad smile.

"Thank you," I looked down at the floor, unsure of what else to say. "We should get inside. The ceremony is going to start in a few minutes."

"After you."

A few minutes later, we were lined up behind the entrance to the room the ceremony was being held in. I leaned forward to sneak a peek.

There appeared to be about a hundred and fifty people sitting in wooden chairs that were painted a golden hue. The sides of the chairs were decorated with light-pink peonies. Those were Olivia's flower of choice. The other two bridesmaids held bouquets of white peonies, which were nearly impossible to find. The color looked great against their lavender-colored gowns.

I reigned myself back in as soon as I heard a violin and piano players start playing a slowed-down version of Regina Spektor's song, 'Fidelity'. It sounded perfect and completely fit the formal setting of Alex and Olivia's ceremony.

Jen and Lindsey were the first to walk down the aisle. They were ushered by two of Alex's family members. Everyone walking down the aisle ahead of me held their head up high and knew exactly when to smile for the photographer. I felt a pit of nerves in my stomach as I silently hoped I wouldn't be the one to trip and fall.

Michael looped his arm around mine, but I pretended not to notice. Step by step we made our way synchronously down the aisle together.

How ironic.

When we got to the podium where the priest stood, we parted ways. Him going to the left to stand with the groomsmen, and me to the right with the other bridesmaids.

The priest raised his arms, indicating that everyone should stand. After a moment of anticipation, Olivia stepped into the room. Her father had his arms around hers and the two of them both looked as if they were going to cry.

What was to follow was a beautiful, albeit long but beautiful, ceremony. The reception was everything I imagined it would be. Grand and over the top, but still approachable. Just like Alex.

Michael and I shared one very awkward slow dance. It was essentially just for show and photo opportunities. The maid of honor and the best man had to put on a good face at their best friend's wedding. After which we spent the rest of the night avoiding one another, even though we were sat at the same table. The best part was I didn't care.

Being with Michael had always made me feel limited in my life. Now that we were over for good, I could feel myself getting lighter. More the girl I used to be before I moved to Manhattan.

After the very last guest had left, I stuck around to help Olivia gather any presents she couldn't carry herself.

"So," I started with a smirk. "How does it feel, Mrs. Carlson?"

Olivia simply looked at me and said, "It feels perfect. Like it was always meant to be."

An hour later I was hailing a cab home and thinking about what Olivia said and if I'd ever have a moment that I would describe as *perfect*.

Hayden and I had been emailing back and forth since graduation. Well, since Michael and I broke up.

Hayden had every right to gloat, to tell me he knew it wouldn't work out with Michael. But he remained kind and supportive. I had told him that I was alright, that I knew I had done the right thing for myself. And I think after the third email, he finally believed me.

I told him about Cassandra's cold email and how she and I would most likely never be friends again. He gave me some spiel about how toxic friendships are never good ones to keep anyway. There was no way for him to know, but I nodded along as I read it.

The two of us went back and forth joking about me coming

212

to visit him in Gainsville. I told him I would, and I meant it. The only problem was, I never asked for his new address. So two weeks after Olivia's wedding, when I had decided to surprise Hayden, I had to stand outside the Ernst and Young office waiting for him to get out of work. That, at least, was something I did know. He'd be out in ten minutes.

I rolled my small suitcase over to the bench in the office's courtyard. Relaxing, I used this time to think about what I wanted to say. The warm Florida air enveloped me and made me feel, just for a second, that maybe this was *perfect*. Maybe this is what Olivia had felt.

But the truth was, I had never been looking for *perfect*. I had always been vehemently searching for *normal*.

At six o'clock on the dot a few people began to exit the tall building to my left. I waited patiently until Hayden finally appeared. Along with a leather shoulder bag, he was wearing dark wash jeans and a polo shirt. Right away I could tell the dress codes were more relaxed down here than in New York. I thought about how nice that must be.

I quickly whipped out my phone and texted, *Look to your right*.

Hayden dug into his pocket and smiled when he looked at his phone. Then he looked to his right, and then locked eyes with mine.

Even in the hot, southern air, I felt a chill. Not one of fear, but of excitement.

I stood up and walked over to Hayden just as he took his first step to walk over to me.

"Hey there," I smiled. "How's it going?"

"What on earth are you doing here?" he replied, a smile tugged at the corners of his lips.

"I came here to visit you," I pointed to my suitcase. "Surprise!"

"Amalia Hastings, you never stop surprising me," he pulled me in for a hug and I stood on my tip toes to reach him. Then I put my hands on the lapels of his shirt and pulled him in for a kiss.

"What was that for?" he asked, nearly breathless.

"For everything," I said, as if it were the most obvious thing in the world. "Hayden, I never should have broken up with you."

"You were confused," he offered, a hurt look in his eye.

"Well I'm not anymore," I declared. "I know what I want. I want you. I want to be with *you*."

Any hurt look had been erased from his face and all that was left was one of shock.

"How?" he muttered. "You're going to Hunter in the fall."

"No I'm not," I said matter-of-factly.

"What?" he asked, the two of us still standing in the same place. "Why?"

"Because I don't want to," I laughed. "Hayden, I can't stand another minute studying. I want a new life."

"Am I crazy to assume that you're taking me up on my offer and moving down here?" he asked slowly.

"My lease is up in a month," I shrugged. "And I think it's time for the next part of my story to begin."

"And for the last part of it to finally end," he uttered, pulling me in for another kiss.

"I actually have a job interview tomorrow at your Alma Mater, Florida University."

I thought about Dr. Greenfield and all he gave up for his career. In so many ways, that story inspired me. It inspired me not to chase after the wrong things in life, like money and power. Or the constant allure of an emotionally unavailable man. Or the thrall of a cold city like New York. Maybe I couldn't make it there. Maybe I didn't care anymore.

"I'm happy for you, Amalia," he reached for my suitcase and started to wheel it down the street.

"Sir!" the doorman from the building Hayden had walked out of was holding something in his hand and quickly making his way over to us. "Sorry to bother you, Mr. Chase, but you dropped your wallet in the hallway."

"Thank you," Hayden gave him a nod and then turned his

attention back to me. "Would you like to come see my new apartment now?"

"I would love to!" I reached for his free hand and clasped it in mine.

We strolled down the nearly empty street and kept on walking all the way back to his place. No cabs, no subway station. Just us, the warm Florida sun, and a new life of possibilities.

The best part? I couldn't think of anything more normal.

Acknowledgements

First and foremost I have to thank all of you, the readers. How wonderful you are for taking a chance on a new author and putting your time and effort into reading their books! You have made it all possible, thank you.

Secondly, I'd like to thank Charlotte Ledger and Kimberley Young of HarperImpulse. These two women took the biggest chance on me and gave me the greatest opportunity that I have even been afforded. They allowed me to take my self-published work and turn it into a three-part series for HarperCollins. Thank you, ladies. I am extremely grateful.

To Dr. James Connor, my former English professor at Kean University. You were the first person who ever told me I knew what I was doing. You were the first person who ever made me feel like I could really be a writer. For that, I am eternally grateful.

I would like to thank my dogs (that's right) Brownie and Cupcake, who forever provide me with love and support. Babies, you are the backbone of this household. Don't let anyone tell you otherwise.

Thank you to Kevin Williamson, Mark Schwahn, Sara Shepard, Joss Whedon, and Julie Plec. None of whom I have ever met, but thank you for writing such captivating stories. Your work has always been my number-one inspiration.

To my family, my friends, and everyone I've met over the past few years who have helped support me with this project. To my sister, Lauren, for actually attending NYU for graduate school and helping me shape the world I've created here. And to New York City itself.

To everyone at HarperImpulse who worked on my books, including my cover designers!

Strangely enough, I'd like to thank my emotions. Although erratic at times, they have provided me with enough creativity to get the job done.

And lastly, thank YOU to that special person for loving me. For making me feel alive again at a time when I never thought I could. And for making me feel things I never knew were possible to begin with.